# Once upon a time

## A Collection of Unexpected Fairytales

Edited by

SJI Holliday & Anna Meade

National
Flash-Fiction
DAY
16th May 2012

In association with SJIHolliday.com &
Yearningforwonderland.blogspot.com

*Some day you will be old enough to start reading fairy tales again.*
*~ C.S. Lewis*

# Contents

Foreword                                                          5

Spotted                          Laurie Theurer                    7
The Lady in the Cottage          Mary Benefield                    8
The Peacock & the Turtledove     Ruth Long                         9
The Monster                      Christine Anderton               10
Once in a Lifetime               Steven Paul Watson               11
I Can Show You the World         McKenzie Barham                  12
No Damn Fairy Tale               Keith Walters                    13
The Ice Maiden                   Anna Meade                       14
Tea                              Jessica Maybury                  15
Running in Heels                 Jo Bromilow                      16
The Storyteller                  A.G.R. Moore                     17
On or Off Course                 Molly Carr                       18
The Box                          Mike Jackson                     19
Red                              Jessica Grey                     20
Beware: Swans                    SJI Holliday                     21
For I Also Need Rescue           Janina Matthewson                22
How to Save a Life               Kelly Lane                       23
Colonists                        LJ McMenemy                      24
I Know                           Victoria Pearson                 25
The Barefoot Girl                J. Tsuroka                       26
Rescued Wolf                     Nanette Pitts                    27
Unexpected Fairytale             Matt Reilly                      28
Pink Bells                       Oliver Barton                    29
Happily Ever After?              Veronique Kootstra               30
The Fairy Figurine               Mark Ethridge                    31
Weaving Lost Notes               Annie Evett                      32
The Shining Vase                 Cath Barton                      33

| | | |
|---|---|---|
| A Mermaid in Texas | Angela Readman | 34 |
| Bad Timing | Chella Courington | 35 |
| Easy Come, Easy Go | Caroline Hardman | 36 |
| The Cinder Princess | Jessa Russo | 37 |
| Not your typical Peter Pan Story | Vicki Orians | 38 |
| Riding Hood | Fayne Riverdale | 39 |
| Deep in the Heart | J. Whitworth Hazzard | 40 |
| The Other Side of the Mirror | Tamara Mataya | 41 |
| The Wind, the Rain and the Ocean… | Lisa Shambrook | 42 |
| Once Upon A Puzzle | Angela Kennard | 43 |
| Just Add | Tracy Fells | 44 |
| Beauty | Sarah Jasmon | 45 |
| Constables | Conor Agnew | 46 |
| The Gift | Barry Chantler | 47 |
| Dust-in-the-throat | AJ Bailey | 48 |
| Wisp | Jonathan Stoffel | 49 |
| The Unexpected Consequences of Inflation | Natalie Bowers | 50 |
| What More Is You Lookin' For? | Erin Ashby | 51 |
| Wistful Wishing | Jenn P. Nguyen | 52 |
| A Moment before Moving | Sarah Nicholson | 53 |
| Pale White | Jonathan M. Wright | 54 |
| Clipboard of Destiny | H. Johnson | 55 |
| Timmy's Escape | Dionne Lister | 56 |
| Rapunzel Had a Bad Hair Day | Eva Rieder | 57 |
| Staying | Annabelle M. Ramos | 58 |
| Unexpected Fairytale | Miranda Kate | 59 |
| The Little People | Leonard E. White | 60 |
| Three Simple Words | Cody Eadson | 61 |
| Skin Deep | Laura Jane Scholes | 62 |
| What Daddy Doesn't Know Won't Hurt | Robert Fyfe | 63 |

Him

| | | |
|---|---|---|
| Cooper and the Death-Cat | Angela Goff | 64 |
| The Thing about Red-Hot Iron Boots | Debra Providence | 65 |
| Otter becomes a Bard | Cameron Lawton | 66 |
| The tooth is out there | Bernadette Davies | 67 |
| Sleeping Beauty Undone | Meg McNulty | 68 |
| Home Cooking | Sara Leggeri | 69 |
| The Blue Garden Shed | Jenn Monty | 70 |
| An Introduction to the Arabika Manuscript Fragment by Professor Conan Floodqvist. (Published in the Journal of Pre-Event Literary Studies, June 2157) | Mark Wilson | 71 |
| Cinderella's Stepmother | Denrele Oqunwa | 72 |
| Fairy Dust Falling | Veronica Stewart | 73 |
| Beanstalk in a Box | Tim Kane | 74 |
| Goethel's Tower | Stacy Bennett | 75 |
| Dragon Tale | Amanda McCrina | 76 |
| A Single Rose | Melinda Williams | 77 |
| A Tale of Morality (or is that Reality?) | Gail Lawler | 78 |
| The Seer of Viceroy | Melanie Conklin | 79 |
| Cinderella 2: This Time It's Personal | Andrew Barber | 80 |
| Just the Ticket | Eleanor Capaldi | 81 |
| Twisted Cinderella | Raiscara Avalon | 82 |
| Maddie White | Jo-Anne Teal | 83 |
| Lost Property | Laura Huntley | 84 |
| The Woman and the... | A. Herbert Ashe | 85 |
| Happily Ever After | H.L. Pauff | 86 |
| The Guardian | Rebecca Fyfe | 87 |
| An Unlikely Fairy tale: We're Going to Disney World | Rachel Stanley | 88 |
| Once Upon A Time | Mike Manz | 89 |

Prairie Wishes                     Eric Martell              90

1002                               L.S. Taylor               91

Fairy Lights                       Jean M. Cogdell           92

God Bless You, John                Afsaneh Khetrapal         93

A Grim Tale                        Daniel R. Davis           94

She Shall Go to the Ball           Sarah Barry               95


Acknowledgments                                              97


Author Information                                           99

# Foreword

I am a story catcher, a word spinner, a teller of tales.

Sometimes I wake late at night, heavy lidded, and my dreams spin out like silvery threads. I pluck at them, gathering the words as fast as I can. Even if I were given a thousand and one nights and as many dreams, I could never tell them all.

Instead, I offer the catchings of others. The Once Upon a Time Writing Contest produced a dazzling array of 88 adapted and original unexpected fairytales, all less than 350 words, beauty and horror in a single page.

You thought you knew the story. This time the wrong person dies. Maybe Hansel and Gretel were actually sadistic brats and Cinderella was a calculating poisoner and the tooth fairy…well, you don't want to know what he does.

Fairytales have power primeval. Many have their roots in ancient mythologies, yet contain cautionary lessons for today: be kind to strangers, respect powers you do not understand, and never ever go in the woods alone.

Enjoy these stories; don't feel guilty. You are never too old for fairytales, to read or to write them. It's never too late to write a fairytale of your own, or to catch a few tales yourself.

Long after we are gone, the stories remain. As long as there are people to tell them, the stories will never die.

*Anna Meade*

# Spotted

*Laurie Theurer*

There once was a zebra named Zed. He was a zebra of the ordinary sort… white with black stripes. He looked and acted just like the other zebras of his herd. He grazed on the sweet grass. He drank at the nearby waterhole. He flicked his tail at flies.

Zed had become bored with his life and longed for something different.

'Why?' asked Zoë, another young zebra. 'We have the perfect life!'

'It's not enough,' replied Zed. 'I want to stand out from the crowd and be different.'

Zed had an idea and convinced two monkeys to help. They met behind the shrubs near the waterhole. One monkey gathered white dust from the dry lake and mixed it with water. This made a slimy white paste, which he smeared all over Zed's body until the stripes disappeared!

The second monkey gathered black stones and ground them into a fine powder. He mixed this powder with water and used his fingers to paint black polka dots all over Zed's body. NOW, Zed felt different and special!

When Zed returned to the herd, the other zebras 'oooohed' and 'aaaahed' at his beautiful polka dots.

Everyone except Zoë. She rolled her eyes and shook her head.

Zed had another brilliant idea.

'Attention everybody,' he shouted. 'Come forward and meet your new king… ME! From this moment forward, you will serve ME. Bring me some sweet grass from the meadow, NOW!'

To Zoë's amazement, the others obeyed their new spotted ruler.

Early that evening, reports zipped among the zebras that cheetahs were approaching their herd.

Everyone was on high alert, except Zed. He was busy giving meal orders, having a polka dot touch-up, and demanding a hoof massage. As the cheetahs came nearer, the herd ran back and forth, attempting to confuse them with their shifting patterns of stripes.

This time, Zoë had the brilliant idea. She maneuvered closer to Zed and whinnied, 'Zed, run!!!'

At last Zed noticed the cheetahs and bolted. Of course, the cheetahs spotted Zed's polka dots immediately. And they didn't mind the taste of the paint.

# The Lady in the Cottage

*Mary Benefield*

The lady sat peering out the window at the dripping trees in her rocking chair of wood. Her face sculpted a solemn look filled with knowledge that could only have been attained through centuries. She rested in front of her television, but her thoughts were deeply placed elsewhere.

As the rain beat against her cottage roof and the chair rumbled across the hard floors, she started to hum a soft tune. Once she began, everything throughout the small room seemed to faintly glow, and all other sounds faded. On the mantle above the fire, the doll with the golden hair looked like it might smile, the top on the floor seemed on the tip of spinning, and the teapot on the table appeared as if it was going to pour itself. Everything within the room had small glimmers of life. The rain began to stop.

Her small notes ended as a motor car parked outside the cottage. The room became dull again, and the rain began once more. A young gentleman jumped out of the car. The old lady carelessly grunted. Edward was always easily prone to panic.

The door swung open. 'They know, Grandmother,' panted Edward. 'Come, hurry, we must go. They know!'

'We shall do no such thing,' the lady said, never taking her gaze out of the window.

'But we must!'

Three men suddenly entered through the doorway. 'You'll be coming with us, Mrs. Morte, and your grandson,' smirked the leader.

'Is that so?' she asked coolly, placing her sharp icy eyes upon them. Beams of light choked the room and then vanished as quickly as they appeared.

Edward stood breathless, his grandmother with a crooked grin on her thin lips. Where the intruders once stood were now three candles.

'We do not run, Edward,' she said bitterly. 'Have I taught you nothing?' Her face returned to the window.

Slowly Edward exited the cottage, never glancing back. As the door closed and he started pacing toward his car, he heard faint humming creep from behind the walls. Sparks of sun light seeped through the trees.

# The Peacock & the Turtledove

*Ruth Long*

I have killed thousands.
I will kill thousands more.
 Blood is my birthright.
 Death my handmaiden.
 Sovereignty my strong right hand.

I am not a man, plagued with conscience. I am an empire, immutable and unforgiving. They say I am mad. What do they know of madness? I did not marry for love nor kill for pleasure. They brought me wives and bid me sow my seed in dry and rocky lands. A lion does not lie down with a lamb except he is tearing it to pieces. He wants for a mate that is sleek and strong and wise. A mind swift and sharp as a scythe. A disposition beguiling as a jasmine blossom. A womb worthy of carrying kings.

I am not a man to be seduced. I am a kingdom to be feared and revered. My subjects tremble before me and my name strikes terror in the breasts of my enemies. I am not capable of wooing a woman. I am a warrior, with bloody hands and heart full of hate. And yet... by Allah, I would hear her call me 'my love' rather than 'my king.' I am not familiar with affection or given to concession, but her companionship is my delight and her devotion my heart's desire and thus, when I take her to my bed this night, I'll speak the words she longs to hear me say.

 Humility is my remedy.
 Love my legacy.
 Fidelity my saving grace.
 I have heard thousands of stories.
 I will hear thousands more.

But tonight the story is mine to tell and this is how it begins: 'Once upon a time ...'

# The Monster

*Christine Anderton*

In that instant, the sheer force of power emanating from the mirror knocked the gathered crowd off their feet, and my hands went up to shield my eyes from the flash of blinding light. I blinked hard to clear my vision. Around me, people were beginning to stand. I stared into the mirror, horrified and disgusted by what I saw. At the sight of glistening teeth, the townspeople screamed, in fear for their lives. She was quick to correct them. 'Kind and gentle,' she said. I leaned in to get a closer look.

I recognized the mirror. I had seen it once before, the night we fled. I stared at the image before me, familiar dishonest eyes glaring back at me in a challenge.

And suddenly I knew. Memories flooded back, pounding me, one after another. Years of being second best. He had always been the favorite, never mind how he had tormented me when they weren't around.

That night years ago, he had behaved as usual, without thinking about how his actions would affect anyone else. Because of him, my life had been taken away from me. He had selfishly ruined everything, and I felt no pity for him. He deserved such a curse. Since then, I had worked hard to become an expert huntsman and had actually made a name for myself.

I pulled my eyes away from the mirror and studied her. Her feelings were obvious. The way she looked at him, the way she cradled the mirror, the way her voice changed when she spoke about him. Kind and gentle? I knew what she didn't. I knew what he was really like. And now he had my girl.

She would marry me. I had asked nicely, but she refused. I wouldn't give up that easily. She just needed a little persuading. I had come here tonight prepared to take either her hand or her father - the decision was hers.

Now I realized that something more stood in my way.

I would have Belle for my wife yet, even if it meant killing my brother.

# Once in a Lifetime

*Steven Paul Watson*

The sobs and moans of the seven echoed through his head like that of a cavalry charging off to war. Deafening, it drowned his thoughts with the exception of a solitary word: why? Heartbroken and numb, still he could not cry.

Someone so perfect, lifeless in his arms. This could not be how it was meant to be. He heard the whisper, he brought his foggy gaze upward, but only a white beard stared back at him.

'Kiss her… love can overcome all obstacles.'

He glanced to the woman still cradled in his arms, limp and without life, so close yet so far away. He pushed strands of her raven hair away, clearing her porcelain face and lips as red as a summer strawberry. In his heart he knew she was the one he had waited for his entire life as he leaned in and softly kissed her lips. Nothing, he kissed her again, holding his lips to hers tasting for a single breath, but still nothing happened. He looked up as the sound of the forest joined in the mourning and he pulled her limp frame to his tightly, as the tears began to fall. It was not to be, he would live his long life, knowing his one true love was lost to him…

…he could smell the aroma of the tea, his mouth watered with anticipation as he brought it to his lips. He opened his eyes, the warmth of the tea still in his throat, his concentration broken by a never-forgotten laughter. He had lived many lifetimes but only once before did his heart beat full of life, a time long ago. He twisted in his chair and looked to each table in the small café to find the source of the woman's laughter.

She had taken her seat only a few tables away, with a book in hand, her long raven hair fallen down around her shoulders. Her blue eyes met his and her strawberry lips formed a smile…

# I Can Show You the World

### McKenzie Barham

The car sputtered, groaned pathetically and died. The road was at a slant and I pulled over with the last bit of juice the old jeep had. The sweat poured but I pulled my sleeves all the way to my palms. I didn't need to see the bruises. Thus far, my escape had failed miserably. And now the nearest gas station was 10 miles away - if I went back to Franklin.

A white truck filled my side mirror, a hazy image against the summer sky. I stuffed myself under the dash, praying desperately, tears leaking. A shadow washed across the jeep. I heard an engine fading and then - silence. I breathed. Something tapped my window. I screamed into my hands, hoping that for once he would lose his composure and kill me.

'Hey, it's all right!'

Unfamiliar voice. I hit my head on the dash as the door opened and I tumbled onto stumpy, dry grass. I looked up. 'You're not... You're not Solomon.' An angelic, unfamiliar, boyish face looked back, wide-eyed.

'No... You okay?' His eyes were deep, chocolate pools and filled with concern.

'No. Yes, I mean, I'm out of gas...'

'Where you going?'

I shrugged. 'Anywhere.'

He nodded his toward his truck. 'I have room.' His truck was piled high with shabby rugs of all shapes and sizes. Otherwise, it looked rather safe.

'You're not going to take me to Solomon?' I couldn't quite believe I was really being rescued.

He smiled. 'Nope. Just offering you a ride.' He held out his hand and gently pulled me up from the ground. I was still shaking.

'I'm Noah. What's...' We both heard it. Police sirens. They had found me.

'They found me.' Noah swore and ran toward his truck. I followed, confused.

'But I ran away... What are you doing?!'

Noah was throwing rugs out of his truck. 'I only need one.' He turned suddenly. 'Do you trust me?'

The first blue siren came up over the hill. 'Yes!'

'Get on.'

He sat down on a dirty rug and winked at me. 'You want to see the world?'

# No Damn Fairy Tale

*Keith Walters*

'This ain't no damn fairy tale'.

She felt the hand tighten around her throat as his rancid breath met her nostrils, her back drawn up sharp against the rough bark of the tree as he shoved her harder.

'So, you can drop the bag - you're not gonna make it to Grandma's house tonight, Snow White!'

Charlotte resisted the urge to tell her assailant that he was getting his stories mixed up, clutched her bag ever tighter, knowing the contents might just save her life. Her feet paddled to seek purchase on the forest floor as she was hoisted higher.

It may have been a human killer that she faced, but his power seemed evermore supernatural.

There was movement in the surrounding darkness, she sensed and then she saw it - figures moving amongst the trees, eyes focused on her. Charlotte didn't fear them, she only feared the man whose hands held her tight, knowing of the trail of corpses he had left in his wake in previous weeks. He'd been hiding right there, in the dense woodland, for nearly a month, his tattered grubby clothing, his growing facial hair more than enough to secure the moniker of 'The Wolfman' which had been anointed to him by the local press.

She waited until she felt the moment was right, stared him right into his bloodshot eyes and spoke for the first time since he'd snatched her from the trail.

'You are nothing.' She raged. 'A nobody - just a killer, plain and simple. Nobody special - for all your huff and puff!'

She kicked hard into both his shins, his hands releasing their grip enough for her to slip loose.

Her hand released the bag, dropping it to the floor. The hardened casing of the police radio inside ensured it wouldn't break.

From the surrounding trees they ran, 14 officers, most dressed in black and with weapons drawn on their target.

DI Charlotte Grimm stepped back quickly as the figure before her raised his hands and placed them behind his head, smiling as he did so.

Charlotte had finally got her happily ever after.

# The Ice Maiden

*Anna Meade*

Greta traced small flowers in the window frost, 'Mother, may I have some cocoa?'

Inge was accustomed to her daughter's formal way of speaking. It'd been a mistake to read Greta poetry, but she hated how mothers gibbered at their babies. As a result, Greta was all precocity at six.

Inge stirred in milk as the wind blew ceaseless at the shutters. After Erik left, she'd scorned moving to her parent's flat in Reykjavik, opting for country solitude. She'd raise her daughter in peace, without interference or superstition.

'A story, please,' Greta had the golden braids and command of a Nordic princess.

'I told you all the stories I know.'

'Tell me the Ice Maiden.'

'On dark, starred nights the Ice Maiden comes, robed in velvet black and crowned with icicles. If you do not leave her a tribute at the hollow tree, she steals under your sill and kisses you with frozen lips.'

Inge knew the words, but was hopeless at the rich cadences her father once infused in them.

Greta didn't mind, listening rapt, 'Then what happened?'

Inge scooped her up, 'Then they lived happily ever after, because it was past their bedtime.'

Once she deposited Greta in bed, Inge snuck to her bedroom for a secret cigarette. She cranked the window open an inch, watching the ash blot the snow on the eaves. Stupid of her to tell Greta that story; she needn't fill her head with dark-edged tales.

The stove was turned too high and Inge nodded off in her chair.

Outside, snow whirled wildly, like they were encased in a glass globe.

Inge woke abruptly. Something had burned - cocoa! She hurried downstairs, pulling on her thin robe. Uneasy, she switched the stove off. Didn't she turn it off before?

Then she saw the open door.

She ran, bare feet crunching unfeeling through ice crust.

'Greta, Greta!' she cried, wind stealing her words.

She found her at the foot of the hollow tree, mug of cocoa clenched in ice-rimed hand, an unclaimed offering.

Inge kissed her daughter's frozen lips, to keep from screaming.

# Tea

*Jessica Maybury*

In 18th century France there was a noblewoman who loved Rooibos more than anything else she put past her lips. It is a tea brewed from a plant that grows only in far-off Africa, and therefore was difficult to obtain in 18th century France. When he was younger and not yet out of love with her, her husband established trade routes ostensibly to traffic in the prized eyelids of elephants, but really to bring his wife that which her heart desired.

However, as the years went by, the couple drew apart and eventually it was not uncommon for the noblewoman to go without sight or sound of her husband for perhaps a week or more.

The court of King Louis XVI flurried up in fictions about where the noblewoman slept at night, the whispers like snow that swirls about only to settle for a time before it is whipped up once more.

The noblewoman grew as distant as the stars, and was rarely seen to smile. She wandered about their grey estates and gardens sipping from a dainty teacup made by a celebrated Italian artist until she passed out of time and mind.

The marquis, her husband, was years later arrested for his writings which documented a fascination with - and perhaps even a life of - sexual violence, sadomasochism and paedophilia. He was incarcerated in Charenton, a cage of cries, and sharp teeth, and despair.

Those trade routes have never faltered, the ones of the elephant eyelids and secret tea. The deliveries have never ceased, the markets never unsupplied.

It has taken hundreds of years but it is only now that Rooibos shortages are being reported.

The press blames the climate.

I know, however, as now you do too, in what forgotten place those decades of leaves can be found.

# Running in Heels

*Jo Bromilow*

*'This station is Once Upon A Time. Change for national rail services to Happily Ever After.'*

Some evening this had been, she thought forlornly, surveying the tattered remains of her tights as she stumbled hazily to a seat. Try as she might, she was yet to come home from even a day, let alone a night, out with her tights still ladder-free, and when your night ends with a mad dash for the last tube at midnight, coinciding with leaving your shoe on the other side of the barrier, you can't expect even 80 deniers to survive. Which these were not.

She looked down at her one remaining shoe with a mixture of sadness and frustration. They were new shoes too - bought on a whim with the remaining fraction of her pay cheque that wasn't ferreted away by the taxmen and TfL. And Tesco. What's a girl to do? She took off the one remaining shoe and dangled it ruefully from her finger, scuffling her now-shoeless foot in an attempt to make it match the other foot for levels of tattiness.

Trust her to book the laziest cab driver in the world - when she said midnight she meant midnight, not whenever he finished his kebab. If prince-like gentlemen at the bar were designed to justify a dramatic 'mystery girl'-style exit, cab drivers were the proverbial gum on the underside of her shoes. Shoe. Another sigh as she contemplated the loss of the beautiful silver pump. She couldn't decide which was more sad - that she'd spent you-don't-want-to-know-how-much on a pair of shoes only to half their value within hours, or that she'd spent the evening flirting and dancing with a beautiful man with a black Amex and then didn't get his number. Opportunity missed there. Some other girl would have got him by now. And she'd never be able to afford to replace the shoes. Oh cruel world. And she'd forgotten to buy bleach to scrub the bath with.

# The Storyteller

A.G.R. Moore

Claudius sat down in the bus shelter. It was a bright day. It was a new day. Much like it was the day it happened to him. His eyes had seen many things; the world had changed so much. He rarely would look in a mirror, but only needed to see the countless wrinkles in his hands to know.

Now was the time to pass it on.

'Mommy, mommy, when's the bus arriving?' He looked up to see a woman and a little girl, no older than seven, sit down beside him. He politely smiled at them both.

'It'll be here soon, dear, now sit down,' said the mother.

'Oh, okay.' The little girl swayed her head, then looked towards Claudius and boldly said, 'Hello!'

'Hello there,' said Claudius.

'That's a big beard!' said the girl.

Claudius could do nothing but laugh, 'Yes, it is.'

'Penny! That's very rude. I'm so sorry, sir.'

'It's no trouble at all, honestly,' he said. Little Penny edged closer towards Claudius, becoming curiouser and curiouser. Claudius held tightly to the ivory head of his walking stick.

'What do you do?'

'Me? It's a secret,' he replied, giving a knowing wink.

'Secrets? I like secrets, I'll keep it, I promise!' she jumped up and down and gave a charming smile.

'You have to promise.'

'I promise! I promise.'

'Okay,' he whispered. 'I'm a storyteller.' The little girl and the mother looked baffled, never hearing such a wild title before.

'What's a storyteller?' asked Penny.

'A father, a brother, a wizard, a hero, a villain, an adventurer and above all a dreamer. Someone who can see hundreds of lives yet live just one. Someone who can spark a revolution. All with a little imagination.'

'Wow!' said Penny.

Claudius brought out his golden pocket watch. The time was 1.05pm. 'I don't have much time but if your mother allows it I'll tell you a story. I warn you though, once told it can never be untold. Once I'm done you must tell it to others.'

'Yes, yes!'

'Are you paying attention? Good. Now, once upon a time...'

# On or Off Course

*Molly Carr*

Being President of the Company was what he enjoyed since decision-making was meat and drink to him. And, of course, he lived like a Prince on his vast income.

Now he was on his way to see the widow of one of his business rivals. It was important to wake her up to the necessity of keeping the firm viable - at least until he could organise an advantageous takeover bid.

Half-way to the house he changed his mind. Neither the business nor the woman would be any use to him. All that it needed was to ask his secretary to send a large basket of expensive flowers, along with a printed message of condolence.

Without wavering - true to himself - he turned the Maserati and made for the nearest golf course.

# The Box

*Mike Jackson*

He was wandering between the shelves, marveling at all the junk, when he heard the voice,

'Excuse me young man. I wonder if you could help me? I'm over here, top shelf, near the back, next to the skulls.'

He looked on the top shelf and there, nestled between some grotesque skulls and two green glass jars, was a small wooden box. Lifting it down and giving it a shake, he whispered, 'Is there someone in there?'

'Yes there is and that someone would be grateful if you would stop shaking him about.'

'Sorry, but I've never seen a box before that's got a person inside it. What are you doing in there?'

'It's a long story. All you need to know is that I'm a Genie and I've been locked in here for a long time. Now if you could just let me out.'

'A Genie! I thought they only came in lamps?'

'Normally they do, but the person who put me in here was in a bit of a hurry and lamps were in short supply.'

'But how do I get you out? There's no lid. Shall I get a hammer and smash it open?'

'Don't you dare! All you need to do is rub the box three times.'

'But that's what you do with lamps? Are you sure it's the same with boxes?'

'What is it with little boys and questions? Just do it!'

'OK, but what's in it for me? Aren't you supposed to give me a wish or something for rescuing you?'

'Get me out of here and I'll give you anything you want. Just stop talking and rub the bloody box!'

'Alright! Alright! But first I have to ask my mum. Mum, can I rub this box three times and let the Genie out? He says he'll grant me a wish if I do.'

'Don't be silly Aladdin. What have I told you before about touching things in shops. Put that box back on the shelf before you break it and come over here where I can keep an eye on you.'

# Red

*Jessica Grey*

No sunlight filtered down through the thick canopy this far into the forest. I listened for sounds of movement, pulling the hood of my mottled green cloak tighter. My red hair would attract attention even in the gloom.

There. The soft sounds of wolves moving through the forest. They drew closer, their panting now louder than the furious pounding of my heart. They weren't hunting, but patrolling, guarding the Coven. Protecting the dark-haired, blue-eyed women who looked as if angels had bent down and molded their forms. But they were anything but holy. We lived in fear of their black magic. Fear and hate.

Every so often men from our village disappeared forever. Sometimes, years later, when the Coven came to trade with the village, you might notice that the children hiding near their skirts seemed familiar. A tilt of their eyes, or a dimple, or chin. You could notice, but you couldn't say anything.

My father vanished when I was young. My mother never spoke of him. But I remembered.

Now it was Liam, my intended. He'd been gone for days. After the first night I knew he wasn't returning. I couldn't just stand quietly and wait for a black-haired witch to have a babe that looked like my love.

The wolves were near enough now. There were two. A young grey and an older wolf with russet fur.

I loosed my arrow, straight and true, into the heart of the grey wolf, catching them by surprise. The red leapt at me, snarling and flashing teeth. I dropped my bow, drawing my dagger. As we collided, I thrust with all of my might. His yelp told me I had wounded him gravely. He fell, and I stood, miraculously still alive, watching his life bleed out.

As his breath stilled he began to change. The fur faded and before me lay a man…one I remembered well although I hadn't seen him since I was a child.

'Red,' the dying gasp came from behind me. I turned toward the big grey, my blood freezing in anguish.

'Liam!'

# Beware: Swans

SJI Holliday

Remember that girl from school? The one with the braces and the stringy hair, the long gangly legs; the flat chest. She was never quick nor funny enough with her comebacks, so in the end she just stopped trying and retreated into her oversized shell.

You meet her again; years later.

Technically, you're middle-aged. Boys are receding and paunchy. Girls are all dark roots and whatever-fits clothes. You all trundle along to the reunion hoping for cheap booze; memories of fumblings behind the bike shed and the day that Jonny Parker set Mindy Collins's hair on fire in the science room.

You don't recognise her at first.

*'Who's that with the tight dress and the smooth legs and the big hair?'*

*'She's talking to Old Beaker, the science teacher. Is she at the wrong reunion?'*

*'She's looks too young to have been in our year - we'd remember her, wouldn't we?'*

Salivating men gravitate like bees to nectar; bitches huddle.

*'Maybe she works here. I don't recognise her, do you?'*

*'Who does she think she is, dressing like that? Showing us up...'*

You look down at the identical glittery tops you've bought from the same High Street store, only difference being some have bought the red and some the blue. No one's bought the black because you're all wearing same style black trousers; cheap polyester-mix straining over inactive rumps.

*'Whatever happened to Mindy Collins?'*

*'Wonder if that bald patch ever grew back?'*

You cackle.

You ladle punch from a bowl the size of a wash-basin, refilling your little plastic cups more often than you take breath.

The woman walks away from Old Beaker and you hear him say: *'Nice to see you again, Mindy. So glad to hear you've done well for yourself.'*

Your mouths hang open.

'Catching flies, ladies?' she says, smiling.

You don't know that she's tipped a little packet into the punch bowl; the crystals dissolved in an instant. Mindy was always good at science.

One by one, you collapse.

In the end, the whole tragic event will just get blamed on the dodgy prawn vol-au-vents.

# For I Also Need Rescue

*Janina Matthewson*

I met a girl who was under a curse, or so she said.

She said that her father was not really her father.

She said that her mother had not really left her. She told me that her mother had been stolen away.

She said that her father, her real father, had been dying and that her mother had gone to save him.

Only, she said, he hadn't really been dying, he'd been taken. He'd been kidnapped in order that her mother would follow, her mother would be lured away.

She told me that her father, the one who was not really her father, was keeping her from finding her mother. He kept her under a spell, she told me, a spell that meant she couldn't speak and be heard, she couldn't tell her story, that what was truth would be seen as fancy or dream or madness.

But there would be one, she said, that would see the truth. There's always one, she told me, who breaks these kinds of spells.

She said there would be a person who would destroy the evil one masquerading as her father and forever set her free. She told me that only when she was free, only when she'd been rescued, would she be able to, in turn, find and rescue her mother.

But, she said, she wouldn't then be free, because, she told me, she would owe herself to her rescuer.

Then she turned and walked away from me and I just let her go.

# How to Save a Life

*Kelley Lane*

He ruined her singledom. Her first night in the city, and bam, she found the guy she would be with for half a decade. It was ridiculous, the same story that so many women her age could tell. First night out in Manhattan and wooed by some pseudo-Mr. Big banker. Unlike the others, she was acutely aware that it would end as tragically as it began. After all, any man that glitters like a Tiffany's window display is not, as one would say, gold.

Luckily, she also knew that it was a matter of time before it happened. Before Mr. Banker sold her like post-bailout Fannie Mae stock and traded for a slightly different model, a waitress, a secretary, or maybe even a masseuse. The plain-Jane seamstress? That she hadn't expected, but she was fine with it. After all, her ex had saved her. Financially, that is. Her car was paid, her student loans taken care of, and her previous salaries from her ad agency job accruing interest. She appreciated him for that and for those years, but it was time to really live. It was time to find real love.

Months later, she was on the prowl. Now the wise hunter that she was, she had done all of the necessary research. It appeared as though they would be infinitely compatible: they both liked eating and walking on the beach, they both had outgoing personalities, and they both liked dogs better than cats. Why hadn't anyone else scooped him up?

In real life, he was far more gorgeous than his online pictures suggested. His hair was as black as onyx, with bright, soulful eyes of amber, marked by flecks of honey gold, breaking the darkness. Her breath caught, he was by far the most beautiful creature she'd ever seen.

'I'll take him.'

'Are you sure you're willing to deal with his medical issues? They can get pretty expensive.'

'That won't be a problem.'

'Then, Ms, you're saving this dog from death row.'

'No, I think this dog is saving me from my jaded existence. Where do I sign?'

# Colonists

LJ McMenemy

Once a jolly swagman camped by a billabong under the shade of a coolibah tree. A few miles away and quite a few decades later, the Stewarts find a shoe while renovating their fixer-upper.

In the deepest, darkest Australian bush, there are age-old practices passed through generations that the Stewarts don't know about. Craig's just removed the shoe from its shelf in the chimney stack; this is a bad idea. He is waving it around at his wife Pippa, who is admiring the quality of workmanship while baulking at the redback spiders that surely dwell within. After all, this place was derelict and all manner of beasties have taken over - and Pippa, though drawn to it, has always had an uneasy feeling inside the homestead.

In the belly of the early settler's house near the swagman's billabong, the spirits are stirring. The house is no longer protected from them by the power of the single shoe. They may rise once more.

Craig and Pippa are preoccupied by their find, so they don't notice the evil eye peering at them through the window. And then the trolls stroll out of the kitchen and make themselves at home.

Craig is too busy staring at the beasties that have invaded his new home to notice what's happening behind him. He doesn't notice the red glow, the fiery heat. He doesn't turn to notice the shadow that was Pippa until she speaks, not with her voice, but with the voice of dark angels.

'Young devilish demons,' Pippa coos. 'What brings you here on this day?'

The underworld creatures bow down.

'My queen,' stammers one. 'My goddess, we do not wish to intrude. It's just - the shoe! It was removed!'

'And you thought it appropriate to enter my domain? Be gone! You are welcome here no more.'

And the underworld disappears; the devil queen makes it so. She surveys her domain. The shoe was removed; the homestead is no longer protected by folk magic.

Nor is Craig.

And his ghost may be heard as you pass by that billabong...

# I Know

## Victoria Pearson

She was never a witch, whatever they say. She was a harmless little old lady and those two demons terrorised her. They stole her pets, hid them from her. Her only companions in the world. I think they killed them you know; I found bones in the garden once, when I was planting potatoes. Their mother was one of those filthy succubus demons. The apple doesn't fall far from the tree.

I know they look sweet. It's part of how they hunt, draw their prey in, I'm certain of it. Everyone that sees them loves them. The twins are adorable with their peachy skin and soft curls. They look younger than 10, don't they?

Remember that boy that went missing last winter? I'm sure now, as I look back, I'm sure they had something to do with it. They were whispering a lot about it, even the boy and heaven knows how difficult it is to get him to speak. She is the mouthpiece of the pair, that's for sure. I don't know where they were the afternoon he went missing. That's all I've got, nothing solid. Intuition.

But I know that woman was no witch. I know she wouldn't lift a finger to harm them, she loved them. She used to stuff them so full of gingerbread that they called her cottage the gingerbread house. As they got old they started playing tricks on her. It got worse and worse. They tormented her, over and over, and yet she always let them back in, gave them their gingerbread. I know it isn't true.

They were never kicked out by their parents either. It's all lies they have made up as excuses for what they did. I shudder to think. Burned alive in your own oven? I actually feel sick. I can't imagine. I won't.

How do I know? I would have thought it obvious, I'll tell you, but you must not judge me on it. They were so tiny, so helpless looking. I couldn't have known what they would become. I am, I am ashamed to admit, Hansel and Gretel's stepmother.

# The Barefoot Girl

J. Tsuroka

Rog knew about the Barefoot Girl.

Sheer white dress, long red hair, pale skin, bare feet.

Her laughter.

She was city legend, whispered among men of a certain... persuasion.

'See her and your ass is grass,' an associate said.

'After everything you've done you're scared of a ghost?' he'd asked.

Rog feared no legend. The city was his territory.

He was out hunting when the Barefoot Girl appeared to him by the fountain in Columbus Circle. She smiled at him through the watery haze and then laughed and disappeared into the crowd.

Her footprints remained on the sun-warmed pavement just long enough for him to track her.

It was now after dark. It might even be the next day.

The Barefoot Girl had led him on a chase all over the city.

They were somewhere in the Lower East Side. Alphabet City, perhaps. He couldn't be sure.

She smiled at him from the mouth of an alley.

'Almost time,' she said.

His hunter's eyes followed her bone-white soles into the darkness of the alley. He fingered the handle of his knife but did not draw it. He never did until it was time to kill. He put on his most lecherous grin and walked into the alley. Rog had spent much of his life in the dark but the darkness in that alley was unlike any he'd experienced.

The city's noise faded and vanished.

Laughter. Rog spun in the dark.

The lights of a passing car illuminated the alley and in that one second he knew where he was.

That name stenciled on the dumpster. That broken fire escape.

A very hard, very cold, foot hit him in the gut.

Laughter. Another kick crushed his jaw.

More laughter. More blows.

The seventh shattered a knee. The eighth broke ribs.

Rog slumped to the pavement.

Laughter. Two pale bare feet, cool against his face.

She reached down and forced him to look, to see his victims - nine women - grinning at him from around the dumpster he left them in.

Laughter. Darkness. Then nothing.

# Rescued Wolf

*Nanette Pitts*

The full moon hung a bit lower tonight. I could hear the howling grow closer with each second that passed. With each howl, my feet became harder to move. I wanted to be seen, be found, be one with them. I was one, but I was alone.

Our kind has always been a myth, never anything people wanted to believe was real. I wasn't even sure I wanted to believe we were real. But I knew they were calling for me. A wolf pack. Tonight I had answered their calls; I let out the howl of surrender.

Once Upon A Time, life had been full of fairy tales. Myths. Happy endings where the prince saves the princess. I never wanted to be the dame whom needed saving. Until I found him. One person that had the ability to see deep into my soul.

William stalked up to me, out of his wolf form. He came to me as a human, because that's how I was presenting myself in the woods. I was not afraid. Though my heart was pounding clear out of my chest. I was afraid he would reject me. His pack would reject me. I needed a pack. I was alone.

I was a lone wolf, I needed a mate. He was alpha male. His choice would be solid. I would be accepted. I needed a strong pack with me to survive. Would he rescue me? I would never admit my distress. I wasn't weak, but I loved him. I could feel his love echo in my head.

We circled each other. Taking in deep breaths of the others scent. He howled and the others joined in, and he shifted into wolf form. His decision was made. I shifted and nuzzled my nose into his neck. He was my Alpha, my prince. I was now his mate for life. I was the lone wolf accepted into a pack, a princess, leader, I was Alpha female.

I needed to be rescued. To be loved. Once Upon A Time, happy endings seemed out of reach. Now, I was living mine.

# Unexpected Fairytale

*Matt Reilly*

Once upon a time
When flash fix did rhyme
A tale did unfold
Needing to be told

This simple story's
Not one of glories
But fighting what's wrong
And just staying strong

No dragon awaits
Beyond castle gates
Our heroes won't save
But they are still brave

A long road ahead
A hospital bed
This is a long quest
To fight for what's best

The evil to kill
Requires a strong will
And strength to abide
The demon inside

For when cancer came
No one was to blame
No sword was unsheathed
No object retrieved

Heroes are lucky
Strong-willed and plucky
Through treatment will stay
To fight a new day

And many do fight
By day and by night
In hope of mending
And happy ending

# Pink Bells

*Oliver Barton*

The pair progress laboriously along the path in the park. He leaning on a stick, each step a pain, she almost bent double, hand in his. She clutches a paper bag. They sit carefully on a bench, very close, avoiding the damper spots. In front of them stretches a sea of pink bells.

It is nine in the morning, and the bag contains croissants. Gertie hands one to Arthur. They nibble in silence, flakes fluttering like confetti.

While a blackbird sings and sparrows edge towards the crumbs, Gertie extends a bent finger towards a plaque half-submerged in the flowers.

'What does it say?' she asks.

'I don't know,' he says, because it is several feet away and his eyes aren't too good.

With a groan, she gets to her feet and shuffles towards it. Bent as she is, she still can't make it out. She retrieves a pair of spectacles hanging round her neck, and peers closer.

Arthur hears her saying something, but his hearing is not too good either. He sees her move forward among the flowers. As she does, she shrinks, smaller and smaller, until she vanishes into the pinkness.

Two sparrows squabble over a croissant crumb and fly off, startling Arthur. He struggles to rise. With his stick, he moves the blooms aside so that he can see the plaque clearly. He expects something like the name of the business that has sponsored this bed, but it simply says 'Come in. Make yourself at home.'

So he steps into the sea of flowers, and at once the pink bells inflate and grow until they are several times his height. The scent is overwhelming, the chime of the bells deep and sonorous. He walks towards Gertie and the others, praying that it doesn't rain. A raindrop the size of a settee would be unsettling. But, he thinks, they must have ways of dealing with that.

Back on the bench, a little breeze sweeps the paper bag off into a graceful dance, an homage, an obeisance, and all is still.

# Happily Ever After?

### Veronique Kootstra

'I'm Terence the Troll and I'm an outcast.'

'Hi Terence,' the group replies in harmony.

Terence looks at the path of cracks he has created on the granite floor. He keeps his eyes on his feet. Juliette the Mermaid is still convinced he wants to kidnap her. If Terence only glances at Belvedere the Gnome he runs away screaming and stands at the door until the end of the session as he can't reach the handle.

'I've been rejected by my family,' Terence says. 'I'll never eat a human. Mum tells the others that I died at birth. I'm scared of going back, but I have to.'

'Thanks for sharing, Terence,' says Avira the Elf, fluttering above the microphone stand. 'Who's next?' How about you, Hendricus? It's been a while.'

Hendricus the Unicorn shakes his head. He slowly walks over to the window. George the Dwarf starts hitting his thighs to the rhythm of the hooves. The rest of the group joins in. Juliette slaps her tail against the side of the bath. Terence stamps his feet completely out of tune. Both go straight through the floor. Everyone stops. Hendricus turns around and starts laughing.

'Ahem! I'll go next,' Princess Genevieve says, as she wipes some water off her face with a silk handkerchief.

'Once upon a time…'

'Genevieve, how many times do I have to tell you? Start again,' Avira says.

'I'm Princess Genevieve and I'm an outcast.'

'Hi Genevieve,' the group replies.

'I didn't want to marry the prince. When he tried to save me, the dragon burnt off all his blond locks. He just didn't look right. I now realise I've made a mistake and will go back today.'

'Thanks for sharing, Genevieve. It's time to say our goodbyes. Can I ask you all to take your potion in your right hand and drink it in one? Good luck everyone. Cheers!'

Terence opens his eyes. He still has his potion clutched in his hand.

*Splash. Splash.*

'I'm scared too.' Juliette holds out her hand. 'We'll do it together.'

# The Fairy Figurine

### Mark Ethridge

The sculptor placed his latest fairy on his workshop table, surrounded by red velvet roses. 'If I got it right, please let me know.' Then he went to bed.

During the night, a fairy came out, and looked at the roses. She smiled, then walked up to the figure. She looked at every detail, touching the figure here, and there. Subtly, the figure changed. Its neck got a touch longer, and more slender. The curve of the breasts got slightly smaller. The corset grew a touch snugger in the waist, and a touch more lowly cut. The skirt split grew up higher on the thigh. The fairy stepped back, and looked at the figure once more. She smiled. The figure looked more alive.

The fairy then took flight. She reached into a bag on her waist, and pulled out a handful of gold dust. She sprinkled that on the figure. The figure's colors came to life. Its clothing looked more like cloth. Its hair grew fine detail that could not be made by hand. The figure's eyes seemed to shine, with real eyelashes, and eyebrows. The figure seemed to smile.

The fairy then flew through the house, to where the sculptor slept. She put her hands upon his lips and smiled. 'I like your work so very much, my friend.' Then she disappeared, as if she never was.

When the sculptor woke he raced to his workshop. With one glance he knew that she had been there. The changes she had made were magic to his eyes. His heart no longer ached, and his soul no longer cried.

He left the figure among the roses. Everyone that visited his shop noticed it. No matter what they felt, anger or sadness, laughter or tears, when they saw that figure, they found their smile again.

Someday the person the fairy meant the figure for would come through his door. They would take it home, and their heart would never ache, or their soul cry tears of pain again, in all the days life gave to them.

# Weaving Lost Notes

*Annie Evett*

Meg perched atop crisp sheets, hugging her knees. Her toes curled, clutching at the material beneath. Shallow breaths refused to be slowed.

Her heartbeat hammered in her ears, drowning out the hum of the air-conditioning and the sound of the floor polisher in the hallway. Sweat beaded on her brow, sliding lazily down the crevices of her shaking body.

Grey shadows reached out from the sides of the walls, their grasping fingers languidly caressing her throat. Meg scrabbled at the stems flowing from her nose, pulling them free. Oxygen hissed, masking the long sliding sounds of ghouls dragging the newly dead up the hall and past her room. Meg squeezed her eyes shut, shutting away the view of the doorway steeped in blood.

Shadows blocked the beam of light under her door. They'd found her. Silver cold dread shot through her body as the door opened. Meg screamed, thrashing as her arms were held by ice cold clamps. Transparent tendrils forced their way into her flailing arms. Red hot pain shot through her veins. Her body softened as she drifted into a blank existence.

'I don't understand how her medication wasn't checked; how her reactions weren't monitored and she was allowed to get to this paranoid state.' The furrowed brow of the crisp white coat bore into the frightened eyes of huddled nurses as Meg's cart wheeled toward intensive care. They scurried off as his physique appeared to fill the doorway. Strikingly handsome, but vigilant and fierce, the newest resident doctor struck terror and had hearts fluttering in all of the staff.

Ned continued to polish the hallway; whilst pushing a heavy bag of laundry periodically with his foot. His dark eyes glinted red momentarily as Meg passed. As her trolley rattled around the corner, Ned frowned as the doctor slowly smiled. The bulge at the back of his coat deflated as his wings nestled back into place. Ned sniffed, acknowledging the victor's possession of the soul.

As the doctor's footfalls echoed away, Ned began to hum, weaving his next dreamcatcher nightmare. The next soul would be his.

# The Shining Vase

*Cath Barton*

I'd picked up the vase in a junk shop in that little town over the Black Hill. It shone at me from the depths of a dusty room on a dank day. I ran my fingers over the surface and it felt like the smoothest skin that ever was. It's a funny thing to say but it seemed alive. It was only when I got home that I realised I hadn't paid for it. I went back the next Saturday, but the shop was shut up and empty. No sign, no nothing. So what could I do?

I do a lot of flower arranging, it's what I love. And the vase was wonderful. It seemed to physically meld with whatever flowers I put into it, enhance their colours and their scents. The more I used it, the better my arrangements.

But one day an annoying thing happened. I had flowers all over the table and the front door bell rang, really loudly. It startled me and I knocked the vase over. All for nothing because it was some stranger asking for Shaylee.

When I'd got rid of the man, told him there was no Shaylee at this address, never had been, I went back into the kitchen and I could hear weeping. The walls are thin and I thought that it must be the kid next door. I put both my hands on the vase to set it upright again and the noise stopped. But something was different. My flower arrangement just wouldn't come right and I felt as if I was in some kind of battle with nature. Flower stems snapped, petals fell off, the greenery wilted and the vase looked sullen.

'Well, so would you be upset if someone had pushed you over.' I whirled round. There was a shining girl standing in the doorway.

'I'm Shaylee,' she said. 'I used to live in the fields here. It's time for us to go on a journey together.'

Shaylee's taken my place, and now that I'm on the other side, she arranges flowers in me.

# A Mermaid in Texas

*Angela Readman*

She don't know why, when she said yes to the legs, yes to the idea of dancing with a guy in a tux, all Fred Astaire, she wound up in Texas. The guy had a motorbike, but that didn't stop her. When she considered dancing it was always old timey, he took off his leathers to Ginger her.

Hot as the devil's fart, she thinks. The air con blinks. She gets beer out the fridge, wishing she could flop inside like a fish. She don't do seafood, makes her sick. It arrives at mini-marts in dusty vans, all the sea sweated out.

She limps down the steps, never got too used to the walking thing. It's too early to stare at application forms. She don't write good. Everything she ever needed to know came in waves.

She sniffs, dips her feet into her paddling pool the kids a trailer over probably pissed in. Bastards, won't leave it alone coz she don't yell - just looks, eyes grey as caught carp.

Sometimes, she misses her voice. It seemed a fair trade. She weren't much using it. Water talked for her. Then, when it didn't, when she got the legs and the man, her mouth got kept too busy to chat. It's good, he said, to be a woman who don't bitch.

Somewhere, on a shale beach lies the conch with her voice in, surrounded. She imagines kids picking it out to take home in plastic buckets. Maybe, someone is holding her shell to their ear. Hears. She wonders if it still sings, likes to think she has a song out there.

The paddling pool stagnates, flies drown. She drags bleach from under her deckchair, pours it in the water and gets in. Sniffs. The neighbours don't speak, hate her, coz she stinks. She scrubs bleach on her thighs and lowers herself, lets it clean the gutted bit between her legs, because she stinks. She knows it. That's why he stopped touching her, never came home.

# Bad Timing

*Chella Courington*

Want your gold ball back?

The Princess came to a halt. A talking frog? Surreal.

Why not. Thanks, she said.

Here's the deal, the frog said. Love me, let me eat from your plate, let me sleep in your bed. And the ball will be yours again.

Like a mannequin in pink organdy with a hem tipped in mud, she stood motionless.

What about a kiss? she asked.

No. I need the whole program.

Don't think so.

With that the princess walked away.

Now the frog started to hop up and down. How can the little bitch refuse me? Doesn't she know the end of the story, how I'd sleep on her pillow three nights and turn into Ashton Kutcher the third morning?

Meanwhile at the castle, the Princess, after a lecture on responsibility and the cost of gold from the King, was given a new ball. She tossed it into the sky, enjoying the way it reflected the sun. At the very moment she let the ball loose, again she heard a croak, startling her. The ball landed on her foot and careened into a thicket.

Hey, pinkee, want that ball back?

I'm not sleeping with you for one ball or two.

She stalked away into the palace.

The frog started hopping up and down. This is my destiny. To follow in Dad's footsteps. The frog gathered the second ball and swelled up his body.

RIBBIT! RIBBIT!

What do you want? the doorkeeper asked.

I seek an audience with the King.

The doorkeeper frowned.

I've got the Princess's gold balls.

A servant carrying the balls escorted the frog into the dining hall. The King and the Princess were eating Escargots Bourguignon.

Who wants their balls back? the frog asked.

Get it out of here, the Princess said.

Egad, the King said.

Things might have turned out as expected, happy ending and all, if Jacques, the Chef de Cuisine, had not come in and seen what all the fuss was about.

# Easy Come, Easy Go

*Caroline Hardman*

As Jamie strolled down the beach the waves lapped at his feet, caressing his bare toes like a girlfriend would. His right arm ached, the raised fleshy edges of his tattoo still pink and raw. It would heal by next week, the guy said.

Sticking out of the sand ahead of him was a wooden post. A handle, Jamie realised as he got closer. He pulled it several times but nothing happened; he dropped to his knees and began to dig around its base until his fingers brushed cold metal.

He stood up and gave a final pull, freeing the object. For a moment he held it aloft then dropped his arms again in shock. Jamie glanced around and tried to look inconspicuous; no easy feat given he'd just been waving a four foot sword around.

A nearby rock caught his attention. He peered suspiciously into his cocktail glass and then checked again. There was no question about it; sitting on the rock was a genie. A freaking genie.

'Best put that back,' said the genie, examining his fingernails.

'No way,' said Jamie, holding the sword tighter. 'I know how this works. I'm not stupid, you know.'

The genie looked at the new tattoo on Jamie's arm; a Chinese character which meant 'arm'. He sighed.

'You're a genie, right? You owe me three wishes.'

'Technically, yes. But there are conditions. No wishing for endless supplies of wishes.'

'How about a wishing tree?'

The genie rolled his eyes. 'No wishing trees. No wishing wells, or magic potions. Those loopholes were closed down years ago.'

'Fine. For my first wish…'

'Something else. Once you let go of that sword, you lose your wishes. You're stuck with the thing forever.'

'Wait, I get three wishes *and* I can keep this sword forever?'

'Yes. You'll be forced to. Good luck getting it through customs.'

'Ah,' said Jamie.

'Exactly. Now, if you have no more questions, I'm off. Once you put the sword back, obviously.'

Defeated, Jamie began digging. Then he stopped.

# The Cinder Princess

*Jessa Russo*

The cinder girl watched him, his brooding darkness so typical, and yet, so intriguing. She kindled the fire absently, unable to focus on the task.

The Prince was unhappy. She could see it in his expression, the tightness in his shoulders. He'd been this way for weeks. She watched through thick lashes, avoiding looking at him directly - she wouldn't risk being removed from his staff.

'My Lord,' asked the soldier, 'does your kingdom not find you well taken care of?'

'Indeed.'

'Do your servants not tend to your every whim?'

'Hmph. Indeed.'

'Then what, sire? What has you tortured so?'

The Prince rounded on him, anger pulling his face.

'Is it too much to ask that I rule my kingdom with beauty by my side?! The human girls keep dying!'

The cinder girl's head shot up. The Prince wanted... love? Of all things! It was preposterous. And yet... something inside of her sparked. A feeling of... no, it couldn't be... hope? She hadn't felt anything for so long. The girl found herself standing up, her body moving without permission, and she, unable to stop it.

The soldier's voice was deafening. 'How dare you approach the Prince!?'

The Prince turned to her, his face softening unexpectedly. When his gaze met hers, she felt weak with the heat of it. Had she still been in possession of a heart, it would have beat rapidly.

He looked at her, not with anger, but with curiosity. Would he strike her? Would she be removed from his charge?

A woman entered the room, unlike any she'd ever seen. All three sets of eyes settled on the intruder, her glistening skin and glowing aura impossible to ignore.

'I see it's too late. You won't be requiring my services after all.' She spoke directly to the girl, completely ignoring the presence of the Prince.

Noting the confusion on the girl's face, she added indignantly, 'I'm your Fairy Godmother. But it seems he's finally seen you. My services you no longer need.'

'But...' the cinder girl said timidly, '...vampires don't have Fairy Godmothers.'

# Not your typical Peter Pan Story

*Vicki Orians*

With the wind at his back, Peter ran toward Wendy's house at a speed that one might suggest he was flying. He knew he had to get away from here. He did not want to spend one more moment in that home for boys, even if it meant he had to grow up and start fending for himself. Peter had only met Wendy the day before, but something about her told Peter that she could get him far away from here.

Peter's footsteps rang loudly as he continued to run through the streets, the only sound in the sleeping town of Nivaland. That is, until the sound of a familiar car came driving up from behind him.

Peter turned to see the black convertible of his warden, Mr. Apindige, flying down the road after him, the squeaking of the tires as rhythmic as a clock. Knowing he stood no chance in outrunning a car, Peter quickly stopped to search for a weapon to fight with. But it was no use.

The car stopped right next to him, and outstepped Mr. Apindige, a baton in his good hand.

'Where do you think you're going?' Mr. Apindige said while batting the baton against his other forearm. He had lost his other hand in a boating accident, and in its place was a prosthetic. It always hurt worse when you were hit with that one.

'Please, don't take me back. I don't want to live in that place anymore!' Peter said.

'I don't think you have a choice. You're just a boy. Now, do what I say, or I will make sure you never make it past 12.'

Beads of sweat ran down Peter's face, and he clenched his fists at his sides, ready to fight. Mr. Apindige was never going to take him back to that place alive. As he was about to swing, a bright, green light appeared next to his face and Peter snapped his head around to get a closer look.

Is that a fairy? Peter asked himself. And then the world around him began to disappear.

# Riding Hood

*Fayne Riverdale*

John was a broad-shouldered man in his fifties, tall and strong, but tempered by age, he lived alone in a small house by the woods. The night was cold, with misty rains layering the world outside in a light frost. John had just settled in for an evening in his chair, when the phone rang.

He answered gruffly, 'Yes?'

'I'm at the cabin, can you come?'

It was his mother but her voice didn't sound quite right, perhaps she was in trouble?

'Ok, I will be there soon.'

John rose and grabbed a torch. He slipped on a blue jumper, pulling the blue hood over his head, as he went outside into the cold.

The woods at night always gave John the shivers. The path wound between great trees that loomed menacingly overhead and no moonlight filtered through the dense foliage above. As John followed the path, the torchlight danced off the undergrowth, small flashes of detail that punctured the dark canvas around him.

The forest around him was quiet, his lightly crunching footsteps the only sound. The night normally brought crickets and owls, the lack of noise made John uneasy. Was there a wolf about? He began to wonder why his mother had called. John pulled his blue hood tighter and quickened his pace.

At the end of the path, the cabin stood, a lit fireplace visible through the window, light and shadow dancing on the porch outside. The warmth was a welcoming thought. John began to relax and walked towards the cabin.

As he stepped up to the front door, John heard a sound. He looked to his left. A small girl was hiding behind a rocking chair, dressed in a red cloak and hood. After a few seconds of surprise, the girl whispered to him.

'Mister, don't go in there, she is not what she seems!'

'Hey?' said John, 'this is my mother's house.'

'Keep your voice down! He will hear us.'

'Oh come on, don't be silly, come in out of the cold', said John.

John reached for the door handle.

# Deep in the Heart

### J. Whitworth Hazard

'Tell me a ghost story, Uncle George.' Patty yawned, her eyes mesmerized by the glowing embers of the campfire.

'Ghost story?' Uncle George kicked his boots out beside the fire. 'Don't know if'n it's a ghost story, but damned if it ain't a scary story…'

'I reckon it was a long while back,' George said.

'Like the 70's?' Patty giggled.

George ignored her sassin'. 'My cousin – Buford - was a poor ranch-hand down New Braunsfel's way, and his wife runned oft with the rodeo, leaving him and his two kids all alone. Now, I don't remember their God-given names - but everybody called them Bubba and Sissy. Their daddy took to Honky-Tonking after they momma runned out, and he fell in with this beautiful filly, name of Tiffani. Buford was in love, because Tiffani had these big ol'…eyes.'

'Big eyes?'

'Never-you-mind,' George stammered. 'Pretty soon, Buford and Tiffani went to the Justice and them kids had a new step-mom.'

'Oooh, was she mean? Did she starve them?' Patty asked, her eyes aglow.

'Damn near,' George hissed. 'She was a VEGAN! Wouldn't let no one have no chicken-fried steak, no brisket, not even… one… drop… of gravy.'

Patty gasped, hugging her pillow.

'Pretty soon, Tiffani had her fill of them step-kids and sent 'em off to summer camp, deep in the woods of East Texas.'

Patty shivered.

'Anyway, Bubby and Sissy skeedaddled from camp to find their way back home. They was plumb lost, and ended up following their noses to an old smoke shack filled with delicious sausages, turkey, and ribs. Well, they got to eating all of it. Turns out it was owned by an old Messican woman with glaucoma, who caught them kids red-handed. She gave them all kinds of Hell, until they tricked ol' Abuelita into the smoker and called the Texas Rangers,' George chuckled. 'When the cops took them home, ol' Tiffani was gone.'

'She died?'

'Worse,' George moaned. 'She left out to liberal-arts college to study Genders… in CALIFORNIA!'

Patty's terrified scream filled the night sky.

# The Other Side of the Mirror

*Tamara Mataya*

Her eyes are lidded lightning. She flashes a white hot glance my way, and I am ruined. Every fairy tale needs a heroine; I made the mistake of thinking it was me. One devastating glance from her shows me I was wrong. Now I can see the view from the other side of the mirror. I've become the ugly step sister. Next to her I become duller. She makes me uglier - on the inside. I want her heart in a box. I want her to prick her finger. I want her to get lost in the woods. I want her to sleep for a hundred years, until I can wake up without feeling inadequate. I want to be back on the other side of the mirror. Back where I realized that everything was perfect in its imperfection. Back where she stood beside me as my equal. Back where she didn't have the cold gleam of triumph in her eyes, knowing she'd robbed me of my happily ever after. There's no trail to lead me back to what I once was. I hate her for doing this to me, and yet I love her still. Everyone's forever on the side of beauty. Even me.

# The Wind, the Rain and the Ocean...

*Lisa Shambrook*

Clouds billowed across the heavens teasing the little sail boat rocking in the ocean's arms below. The sailor glanced skyward and Rain offered a light-hearted shower, her watery robes glistening in the sunlight.

Wind whipped her skirts about her and hurled her sister a glare interrupting the sprinkle. 'You won't win like that!' she hissed sending her own provocative sigh into the little boat's sails.

'Well you're not doing any better!' said Rain resuming her shower, crystal raindrops shrouding the wooden mast.

Wind swept out her hands and blew her sister's fluffy clouds away, scattering her sparkling drizzle across the sea. Wind smirked and pitched a gale. Her long hair fluttered in the remnants of the storm and Wind sent a swirling gust to envelop the sailor amid the violent squall.

Rain clapped her hands, darkened her clouds and her torrents engulfed the boat.

Wind whipped up a fury. 'He'll be mine, not yours!' she shrieked, her temper flaring as rain poured.

The drenched, shivering man on the deck below cursed them both as the tempest arose.

Wind, determined to beat her sister, stirred up a whirlwind and coiled her tendrils around the sailor, but Rain wasn't to be outdone and let her roiling clouds release their cascade in a waterfall of tears. The valiant sailor fought as howling wind swept his boat awry, and torrential rain flooded the deck leaving him clinging to the rail of his boat.

The storm flourished as Wind and Rain battled conjuring up blazing lightning and ear-splitting thunder... and as they did, waves swirled and churned beneath the tiny boat, booming against the bow and hurtling across its deck. Beneath the keel Ocean smothered a chuckle and allowed her sisters' fight to escalate. Their ensuing wrath would assault her in vain but their prize was hers.

Ocean tossed her white hair as it danced on the waves and drew the little vessel beneath the spray. The sailor slipped into her grasp and quietly acquiesced within her embrace and kiss... after all, she knew what her sisters didn't – a sailor always gives his life to the Ocean.

# Once Upon A Puzzle

*Angela Kennard*

'Mom?' Adam whispered.

Adam's wide eyes scanned the cramped space, a beat-up desk, two chairs - one wobbly, one with duct tape across its center - and scuffed yellowed linoleum. Huddled against a grease-stained wall, Adam searched for his mother. One moment, she'd been sitting at the desk working on a jigsaw puzzle, while telling him a story about a panda bear who'd lost his teapot and had to travel from China to Australia to steal it back from a pesky kangaroo, when poof, she'd vanished.

His mother had been driving him to school that morning when their tire had blown out. They'd found themselves stranded in front of an auto shop. A man covered in grease and smelling of gas had ushered them into the waiting room. He'd grunted indiscernible words and disappeared through the only door in the room. Seeing a half-finished puzzle on the desk, Adam's mom started working on it, while Adam slumped in a chair.

Panic caused Adam's heart to pound, his hands slick, his mouth dry. The windowless room pressed in on him, the air stale. His ears hummed and the tang of acid filled his mouth. A tear slipped down Adam's cheek and he brushed it away. He straightened from the wall with a quick jerk.

Light pulsed from the table where he'd last seen his mother. Adam's feet dragged as he walked toward the table. The light wasn't coming from the desk, but from the completed puzzle. Adam's body shook as he reached out a hand toward the puzzle. He wanted to stop himself, but couldn't. His fingers brushed its corner.

'Adam!' He jerked his hand back, cradling it to his body.

He glanced around the room, his eyes wild. He'd heard his mother yell his name. But how?

'Mom?' Adam reached out once more, laying his palm flat on the puzzle.

'Adam, run!'

Adam's hand fused with the puzzle. He gasped and bumped into the desk's chair, which landed with a crash. The light of the puzzle faded as the door creaked open and laughter filled the empty room.

# Just Add

*Tracy Fells*

Miranda munched the last triangle of toast. Her diet required thirty chews before swallowing but it wasn't a chewing sort of day. According to her horoscope it was a love day, as she should 'Expect a romantic delivery'. Miranda had little faith in astrology. Goat's intestines were more reliable, but the neighbours complained about the smell and virgin goats were hard to come by.

Miranda's mouse squealed as she clicked on the tracking tab of SpellsRus.com. Her parcel was scheduled for delivery at 10:28 that morning. The digital timer on the cauldron read 10:27. As the glowing number seven blinked into an eight the doorbell chimed. Miranda shivered, a coy smile flirting behind ebony eyes.

She skipped to the door, snatched the package from the startled postman and then scuttled back inside like a giant black beetle.

A mottled brown frog and a sheet of paper tumbled from the padded envelope. Miranda quickly scanned the instructions, eager to begin. Kissing was so old style. All she needed was a drop of water. Pure sparkling would be best, she thought, and opened a bottle of France's finest.

'Ribbit,' said the frog and disappeared in a mist of emerald smoke. When the smoke cleared, a tall, tanned handsome man stood before her.

'Pardon,' he croaked, 'but my belly eez full of bubblez.'

Miranda turned over the instruction sheet. There was a miniscule warning hand written in blood-red ink. Carbonated water can cause premature eructation.

For a fleeting heartbeat Miranda held her breath and then Prince Charming exploded with a mirror-cracking belch, splintering like a waterfall of diamonds across the lino.

With hands on ample hips Miranda expelled a rude charm.

A cough from behind her announced the postman's return. In haste Miranda had left the front door swinging. 'Sorry pet, forgot to give you this – it fell out in the van.' He held out a container of liquid.

Miranda appraised him. Not bad looking, quite charming in fact. She welcomed him into the steaming kitchen. His trainers splashed in the puddle. 'Don't worry,' she cooed, 'it's only water.'

# *Beauty*

*Sarah Jasmon*

Once upon a time, she sat in the confines of the tower chamber, watching in her mirror as the colours of the setting sun gave back to her hair the illusion of body and colour. The moment always passed too soon: as the last golden strand faded and disappeared, she reached up a thickened fingernail to scratch at her scalp. The young man's face on the far side of the tower registered a look of disgust. She was past disgust. The gentle flakes hovered in the air: she liked to see them dance.

'If you marry me, you will gain riches beyond your wildest dreams.'

His chin tilted as he rejected the offer with silence, his eyes fixed on the distant horizon.

'If you marry me, your power will stretch to the mountains and beyond.'

Again, silence.

Her voice she disliked, the weakness, the wavering lack of cadence. At first, she had tried to exercise, to sing the phrases taught to her by the court musicians, but still her vocal chords had twisted and hardened like the roots of a petrified forest.

The line of the boy's jaw was visible in the encroaching dusk, taut, smooth, the beautiful line sweeping down from his perfectly formed ear before curving upwards towards the dimple in his princely chin. Was there, perhaps, the hint of a tremble in his rigid mouth?

'You dream of conquest, of mighty deeds, of valour. Look beyond what you think you know, and it shall all be yours.'

The tiniest shake of the head gave his response.

No matter. She herself would age no more. She could sit and watch as his hair, too, became thin and leached of colour, his joints thick and his eyes misty. In the end, he would agree. And in the meantime, the evening glow would continue to bring its moment of illusory youth, whilst the early rays of the morning sun would daily strike the mirror and reveal, for the briefest moment, the shadow of the beautiful girl within, awaiting her release.

# Constables

*Conor Agnew*

'So, (belch), so that's it? Hmmmm?' Leaning in with intent, Hank stared with one eye wide and protruding, the other in a sort of confused squint, trying to coax a response from Bronson, currently distracted by the nutshells he flicked lethargically across the bar as the days events traced themselves across his vision once more. Four weeks suspension, with pay for two. How would he explain this to Rose? Not that she hadn't seen it on the news already, or heard about it in texts of hysterics from the other constables' housewives.

'So we take our eye offa his Lordship Dumpty... for FIVE seconds, and he... he falls on his arse quicker than our Bertha af'er a ni' on the piss.' Hank wiped away the excess beer from his face, his words beginning to trail like the stain drawing itself across his sleeve.

'Five seconds', Bronson echoed. 'How did he not jump that wall? It was two feet, hardly a bloody obelisk now, was it?'

'Obawhu?'

'Nothing', Bronson sighed. 'Finish your pint, bar's closing', pointing at the clock.

The innkeeper rang for last orders. An inebriated smile stretched itself across Hank's face.

'That's wha' I like about you, Bron-boy', said Hank, flinging a friendly, albeit sweaty arm, across Bronson's shoulders. 'Ed-ya-cated, never... never shy to face up to anyone. Eh? Eh? Inspector King, he near had a heart attack when you tol' him what happen, haha! You see the look on 'is face!?'

'I did, yeah', replied Bronson, wanting to subdue the show-reel in his head. A broken ankle. Fractured wrist. Fractured cheekbone. Cracked elbow. What puzzled Bronson was how a man could inflict so much damage on himself from one measly fall.

'Still', Hank raised a hand, calling for a last pint of ale, 'boy shoulda kept his glasses on, keep 'is eyes front. Lords, eh? Wassa point? Fat men with no sense, I say. (burp) What kinda name is Dumpty, anyhow?'

Bronson remained drooped over his beer, listening wearily to the last few chairs being placed on the tables as the evening drew to a close.

# The Gift

*Barry Chantler*

Every mid-summers eve, my Irish grandmother would put bread and milk in the garden for the little people. The offering was always taken. My grandfather would scoff saying, 'All you've managed to do is feed the hedgehogs.'

Me and my brother wanted to see the fairies, but knew there was no chance being allowed to stay up late to watch. So one year, when I was seven, we smuggled in the bread and milk and placed it in a corner of our bedroom; then kept sentinel.

I must have fallen asleep because I awoke much later to a pitch black room. Faint glimmers of blue and gold sparkled in the shadows. I sat up and there on a bedpost danced a tiny silvery figure formed from sticks. After a while it vanished.

Then I dreamt I was a badger pushing through undergrowth under the milky sheen of a full moon. I could feel the thorns in my fur; smell the fresh soil as I rooted round, so vivid, so real.

Then I floated up near the ceiling, looking down on my sleeping form. I drifted through the door along the landing and down the stairs. Though I couldn't see anything with me, it didn't feel like I was alone. I floated out into the garden and towards a streetlamp, where I careered round like a moth.

Then I woke and it was morning. The bowl was tipped over and empty, the bread had gone. Our bedroom door was shut all night and we didn't have a cat. You work it out.

When we told my grandmother, she became distraught, saying: 'you should never invite the little people into your home.' She gave us each a rabbit's foot charm and made sure we carried it at all times. And she continued every mid-summers eve to leave out bread and milk. And every year the gift was taken.

'Just hedgehogs,' my grandfather told us.

But, you know, I'm not so sure.

# Dust-in-the-throat

*AJ Bailey*

May I suck at your elbow before the plaster? asked the gnarled little man of the first donor. No, said the donor, what is left is for me and what they take will be used.

May I suck at your elbow before the plaster? asked the gnarled little man of the second donor, I will give you my shoes in exchange. I do not need your shoes, said the second donor, and what blood they leave me is mine.

May I suck at your elbow before the plaster? asked the gnarled little man of the third donor, I will sit on your chest and groan if you say no. You are too light and too quiet to worry me, said the third donor, and I must look after my blood.

May I suck at your elbow before the plaster? asked the gnarled little man of the fourth donor, I will marry you softly in moonlight if you only say yes. I fear I am as spoken for, said the fourth donor, as the blood that hasn't been given will be.

May I suck at your elbow before the plaster? asked the gnarled little man of the fifth donor, I don't know how else to ask. Your name is not Parchibald, said the fifth donor, nor is it Chupacabrachups, but Dust-in-the-throat should be gone. And Dust-in-the-throat wailed as the gnarled knots of his joints riddled themselves fine enough to float out of the ward on a breeze that sprung from between the biscuits and the tea urn as if for no other purpose.

# Wisp

*Jonathan Stoffel*

A garbage truck jangles over the bridge behind him. He nearly leaps off by reflex.

No.

It must be a decision.

It seemed a difficult decision moments ago, but now exhaust clogs his lungs. The biting of concrete saws pierces his ears. She swore she would never leave, and he buried her.

He stares down into the abyss, wondering if it holds any more comfort.

She had been different, like him, a perfect pairing. She had told him she would go, yet remain. He had not believed.

A light breeze brushes his cheek, and his gaze follows a blue butterfly away from the pit, toward the horizon. The wind brings faint whispers, a language foreign to him, though she had claimed to try to teach him. To prepare him, she said.

He had played along, knowing it to be just one of her eccentricities.

Was it?

The butterfly disappears into the boughs of her so-called sisters, and for a moment, the construction crews cease, the traffic stops, and he strains to listen.

The rustling tongue is still unfamiliar, but somewhere in the hissing, he almost hears beckoning, urging. Pleading, even.

The lives of those around him resume, and yet he still hears the almost-words. A scent of honeysuckle drifts over the stench of burning oil.

A tear slides down his face. She had taught him to taste the sweet flowers.

He closes his eyes and basks for a moment in the soft wind, the sunlight embracing him.

With a sigh of resolution, he heaves himself over the guard rail and walks back to his home, his garden, his love, who - though now only a sapling - will keep her promise to be with him forever.

# The Unexpected Consequences of Inflation

*Natalie Bowers*

One by one, D.I. Stringer slid the photographs across the table and lined them up in front of the suspect. He watched for a reaction, but the smug little git just kept smiling.

Stringer tapped the first image. 'Kirsty Wilkins,' he said as steadily as he could. 'Seven years old. Found by her mother on February 26th. She thought her daughter was sleeping late. Until she pulled back the duvet.' In his 20 years on the force, Stringer had never seen anything like it. The suspect, though, seemed unmoved.

Stringer grit his teeth and tapped the second picture. 'Little Alex Fletcher. Six years old. Found by his mother on March 29th. She thought he was sleeping late too. Until she drew back his sheet.' As the first officer on the scene, Stringer had been the one to prise Mrs Fletcher from her son's body. The noises she'd made would haunt him forever; it'd sounded like someone had taken a razor blade to her soul. The suspect, however, appeared unaffected.

Narrowing his eyes, Stringer nodded at the third photograph. 'Hwyl Davies. Only eight years old. Found by his mother on April 28th. Same story. Until she rolled him onto his back. Until she saw what you'd done, what you'd taken.' Although the memories turned Stringer's stomach, the suspect's expression still remained unchanged. Stringer clenched his fists. Bloody immigrants. They didn't give a crap about anyone but their own kind.

'Look!' He thumped the table. 'Forensics puts you at all three scenes. Dust found on the windows matches dust we found on you. And the little tokens you left behind? Your fingerprints are all over them. I know you did it. I just don't know why!'

Finally, the suspect's smile faltered. 'Kids these days,' he said. As he shrugged his shoulders, the tips of his wings fluttered. 'Selfish. Each time they lose a tooth, they demand more and more money. But teeth don't fetch what they used to.' He laughed. 'Internal organs on the other hand...'

# What More Is You Lookin' For?

*Erin Ashby*

A limo pulls up in front of the new aquarium.

In the backseat, Nick's mother straightens out her cocktail dress. Nick's earbuds are blasting some thudding trash. She leans over to straighten his tie. He slaps her hands away, flipping her off as he crawls out the door.

He shoves his way past old rich hags in diamonds and elbows a photographer in the stomach.

His dad is CEO of Bex Oil. Nick doesn't know what CEO stands for. He does know something about the beach. His dad is killing the beach, destroying the earth, collapsing the universe. Or whatever. His biology teacher gave him nervous looks when they did papers on environmental issues. Every kid in class talked about Nick's father. But Nick knows his dad is an asshole. He heard the aquarium is some bone to throw at green people.

He snags booze and sniffs out an intern with shaggy hair who's most likely holding. On a catwalk over a massive tank, Nick is stoned right into the floor and guzzling Dom Perignon. The intern is babbling about selling out, Greenpeace, college girls... Nick lies on his stomach and leans over the water. There are tiger sharks in there, and manta rays, and other freaky creatures. There are also stone statue things covered with barnacles and shells. Nick blinks into the depths. He can't even see the bottom. There's something in the corner of his eye...

He squints. Can't see it straight on. Something out of sight... Boobs?

He sees boobs. Almost. But he can't quite look at them. Weird? Boy, is he high.

He hears a whisper and since he feels like he's floating anyway, he pushes himself off the catwalk and into the blue, as the whisper becomes a waterlogged scream.

It's three o'clock in the morning and their impossible, no doubt rehab-bound son is vamoose. The mother growls obscenities and frowns into the manta ray tank, thinking that an ugly as hell little stone formation shouldn't be blocking the pretty coral.

What dumbass put that there?

# Wistful Wishing

*Jenn P. Nguyen*

I once thought that once upon a time meant that I would get a happily ever after. That no matter what happens - that whatever crap lands in my hellhole of a life - somehow things will all turn out for the better.

I couldn't be more wrong.

'It's too bad you couldn't come to the ball, Cinderella,' Anastasia said with a triumphant sneer. 'The prince couldn't keep his eyes off of me.'

Stepmother pinched her thin cheek and beamed with pride. 'I just know he'll come calling on you soon.'

'Of course. He has to return my shoe after all.'

I stumbled backwards in a blurry haze. 'I'll get you your tea.'

No, this wasn't supposed to happy. I was supposed to go to the ball and meet the prince. To fall in love. This was supposed to be my reward for being kind all my life. She wasn't supposed to charm the prince. She wasn't supposed to live out my dream.

Yet somehow, in some way, she did. She will.

It wasn't until then that I knew happily evers don't come for free. I'd have to work for my dream, my future.

It took me a few minutes to prepare their tea. Only a second to pour in the arsenic.

Later, I hummed a little tune to myself as I washed the dishes. A dream is a wish your heart makes. When you're fast asleep…

Thud. The first thump came from directly above my head. I didn't even look up, still continuing with my chores. After I wiped my hands on my tattered apron, I picked up Anastasia's sparkling blue mask and brushed at the invisible dust. Thud. Another one. This time from the bedroom above the dining hall. Barely noticing, I fastened the mask on and brushed a few blond tendrils off my face. It fit perfectly.

Thud. The final thump was the loudest of them all.

Finally I allowed myself to smile and settled on the wooden chair with the glass slipper in my lap. Now I'd just have to wait for my prince to come.

# A Moment before Moving

*Sarah Nicholson*

'Someone who loves you very much must have given you that.'

Saffron thought the words were only memories in her head but turned around to find a young man in navy overalls standing beside her. Must be another removal man, she reasoned, his face looked familiar although she couldn't quite place him.

'My husband used to say that.' She couldn't stop the stray tear escaping as she remembered being carried over the threshold, wrapped up in lace and love.

The man beside her offered a folded white handkerchief; it almost shone in the sunlight.

She dabbed her eyes and passed it back to him.

'Keep it.' He said softly folding her fingers round the soft cotton with his own, almost knowing she would need it again before this day was through.

She had often wondered, late at night, alone, what it would feel like to have another man touch her, even just as innocently as this. There was no shiver down her spine nor recoil; his touch was natural and kind.

Trying to avoid his eye she stared at the handkerchief. There was an X monogrammed in the corner.

'Xavier?' she enquired, finally daring to look up. She couldn't think of another single name beginning with X.

'Must have picked it up somewhere on my travels.' His grin was cheeky and his eyes sparkled.

They looked at one another for what seemed like eternity. Even the air held its breath as a myriad of memories tumbled round her head.

'I hope you'll be really happy in your new home Saffie.'

He disappeared as softly as he arrived leaving her to wonder how he knew her first name. It wasn't fair when he had never even told her his ... but perhaps she already knew.

She looked again at the handkerchief. Maybe it wasn't an X after all but a kiss.

'Someone who loves you very much must have given you that.'

# Pale White

*Jonathan M. Wright*

He stuck his head out the window and peered towards the quiet forest. His dark hair glistened and his blue eyes glowed in the pale moonlight. Only seconds ago a noise erupted deep within. It sounded like a girl's cry for help, but it stopped as soon as it started. When he didn't hear the sound of the crickets chirping or the owls who-ing, the young villager became distressed.

Hopping out the window, he ran into the darkness of the forest and called out: 'Is anybody out there? Are you okay?' He stopped a few feet past the tree line and tilted his right ear, listening for any signs of life. Far off, the sound of leaves rustling caught his attention. Then, he heard a faint yelp.

Dashing towards the noise, the villager tried to keep an eye out for any signs of the girl. Sadly, the light of the moon couldn't fight through the canopy of the enveloping dark woods. Stopping for a brief second, he called out again: 'Miss, are you hurt?' No reply. Instead, he searched around in all directions hoping he hadn't passed her. In one direction, he saw the glow of a tiny bug illuminating the face of a young woman dressed in white.

The young man ran to her and knelt beside her, looking for any wounds. 'Miss, are you alright? Can you hear me?' While he checked her body, he noticed her hair and skin were pale, paler than the moon. Her skin almost gave off its own glow.

The woman sat up and opened her eyes to reveal glowing orbs. She opened her mouth and screamed while staring into the man's face. He stared back in utter shock, unsure of what he was seeing. He, too, opened his mouth and began to scream, but it was overpowered by the eerie girl.

The young man lay on a stone altar while the other villagers surrounded him and wept. An old lady passed holding a handkerchief, tears falling down her worn cheeks. 'Why didn't he listen to the tales of the banshee?'

# Clipboard of Destiny

*H. Johnson*

I deposit my silent screams in the basement file room. Few of my coworkers have the key, and fewer want to visit the rank, dismal bowels of the old newspaper building. Most importantly, Judy never goes there. Last Friday, I sat in my usual spot by the 1994 tax information. I inhaled deeply, opened my mouth wide, wrinkled my nose, and squeezed my eyes shut. As I quietly exhaled, releasing thirty-six hours of frustration, I heard sniffling. Alarmed, I skulked past rows of moldy boxes toward the sound. A tiny woman slumped on a step stool near the 1983 personnel files. Her orthopedic shoes barely touched the floor. Glaring at me from behind enormous purple-rimmed glasses, she dabbed at her nose with a handkerchief. 'It's a good day for this room,' she said.

'Sorry, I didn't realize anyone was down here,' I mumbled.

'I'm retiring today,' she said, slipping the hankie into her pocket. When I could see her whole face, I estimated she had seen the advent of moveable type. 'Not by choice. But they can soak their heads. I have books to read. Cats to feed. Magic to make.' She snorted.

'They say you're busier after retirement than before,' I offered, making a noise like a little laugh.

'Here,' she stood, scarcely taller than when she sat. A wing-shaped rhinestone comb held her gunmetal updo in place. She pulled a silver glitter-encrusted clipboard out of her coat and shoved it at me. It was heavy. 'This will help,' she sighed, ambling away. I skimmed the parchment clipped to the board and immediately understood. I smoothed my hair and made my way back upstairs. At my desk, I studied the form. Everyone in the office was listed on the left. On the right side, a hundred phrases were each accompanied by a blank box. I circled 'Judy' on the left side. My pen lingered over 'vacation,' on the right side, but then I saw the best choice. 'Colon polyps.' My checkmark was bold and dark. I clasped the clipboard to the ink stain on my shirt and grinned.

# Timmy's Escape

*Dionne Lister*

Tim hid under the wharf. His parents stood above, he could see the soles of their shoes through the small spaces between the timbers. He had escaped to this shadowy space, when his parents had started shouting at each other again. He drew squiggles in the sand with a stick, water lapping at his feet.

Venomous words reached him, their hate wringing tears from the young boy. He dropped his stick and pushed his palms over his ears. Staring at the water, but seeing nothing, he chanted quietly, 'Please take me away, please take me away.' Almost unnoticeable at first, he heard a flute. The notes enticed him and he dropped his hands. He focused then, and felt the notes brushing against his skin; a warm caress, and then he saw her.

A faery emerged from the water, her skin shimmering silver, her eyes dark pebbles that have lain on a riverbed for millennia. She smiled at him and her voice slipped in between the flute melody:

> *Timmy swim with me,*
> *To a life of serenity*
> *Under the sea.*
> *Timmy hold my hand,*
> *I will show you peace*
> *Where your smile will be free*

Donna looked at Frank, cursing him under her breath, I hope you have a heart attack and die, right now. Frank shook his head, another out of control fight, another pylon taken out of their relationship; they were about to collapse and he knew he would be the one to lose the most. He would lose Tim.

Frank blinked, 'Where's Tim?' In a moment neither one would ever forget, they realised he was not there. Frank found Timmy's sneakers under the wharf. When he tipped them upside down, silver glitter floated to the ground.

Flute music haunts their sleep and Tim's parents dream of a woman, black eyes deep and mocking. She holds their son, his blue face reflected in her silver skin, his hair floats this way and that, with the underwater currents, and his mouth smiles at something only his dead eyes can see.

# Rapunzel Had a Bad Hair Day

*Eva Rieder*

They say Rapunzel had the longest hair. What was she in? A tower of some 73 feet?

Well naturally, I found my way to that tower, chest puffed and neck straining, and stared on up that ungodly height to the little face peering out at me. I slayed the witch yesterday, so it seemed I had a fair chance of making it up to my Princess.

'Rapunzel, Rapunzel, let down your—'

'Got it,' she screamed, and down came the tangled mess of hair.

I suppose I should understand that a gal trapped in a tower with a mane almost 73 feet long is worth waiting for, but that's a pretty long climb on a lot of split ends. I didn't really believe it until I started climbing, Rapunzel bitching almost the entire time.

'Ow. Ow. That really hurts.'

'I'm the Prince, Rapunzel!' I said, but she kept on whining.

When I approached the top, the tension grew ever tighter, and her bemoaning of the situation ever louder. I had to ask myself, what kind of Princess gets herself trapped in a tower?

And did she bathe?

So it was as I tossed myself over the window ledge that I slowly peeled open my eyes, Rapunzel cranking her hair back onto her head with some sort of pulley system and fussing as if she had a head big enough to house this dreadlocked mess. But really she had a pinhead. A pretty little pinhead, but not one befitting that length of hair. She smoothed her hands along her dress and smiled - you know a girl trapped in a tower hasn't seen a dentist, right? - and I just scoped it all out with a sigh.

'I've come to rescue you, Rapunzel.'

'Oh Prince!' she squealed. She looked a tad on the old side, really, but I guess she'd have to be to have that hair. She wrapped her gnarled hands around my neck, and when she planted her kisses over my face I resolved first thing we'd get her teeth cleaned.

'You saved me!'

Oh yeah, I sure did.

# Staying

*Annabelle M. Ramos*

'Remember that time, when we were 12?' He gazed into her honey-colored eyes. These were the same mysterious eyes that captured him when they were younger. Many years had passed since then. But his heart hadn't changed.

He would have walked to the ends of the earth for her. Although he didn't need to now, because she had been the one to cross the seas, leaving her homeland, to return to him.

'Yes. Of course I remember,' she breathed. Her father, the King of her land, had taken her along on his journey. Far away from the familiar sand dunes and houses made of wheat-colored stone. To a place where fields were green, and luscious, and covered in mighty, ancient trees. This was the place where she found him - the other half of her soul. Even at that young age, she already knew.

The princess and the boy she'd loved her entire life lay together now, on the soft ground of this secret forest. On the same spot where everything began. It was still hidden, behind bold, copper mountains, and still serene, with only the fairies and fireflies for companions.

'Let's just run away,' she said. She had suggested this a thousand times in the past, over their secret letters.

'No,' said her beloved. 'This must be done.' He untangled himself from her and looked to the heavens for a sign. The fairies and fireflies gathered around them, illuminating the branches and leaves of their fortress. 'See,' he said. 'These fairies bring us luck. We'll be together for always, when tomorrow is complete.'

The next day, the three of them gathered in a wide meadow - the princess, her love, and the prince to whom she was betrothed.

The princess lowered her eyes and prayed that her beloved would triumph in this duel. A fight to the death for her hand.

But in the end she learned that fairies brought no luck. The prince left her on her knees, as she wept and her silk garments soaked up the blood that once belonged to her love. And then, the vultures came.

# Unexpected Fairytale

*Miranda Kate*

Lori stroked the cover of the book; a special edition copy of Cinderella. It had signs of age; the edges of the dust jacket were worn and the spine faded. But when she opened it and saw the inscription inside, her heart lifted; 'I'll be your Prince any day of the week!'

He had known how much she'd loved the story from the first evening they'd met, and how it had inspired her to become a children's author. And when he had given it to her the night before she had left his country, it had encapsulated so much of how he had healed her. He had listened to her, considered her, thought about what she might like and acted on it. No one had ever done that before. That's what had made him so special. And despite the fact her visa had run out, and that he was far too young for her, they had made a deep connection.

So it was no real surprise some 12 years later, while she was suffering again in a marriage where there was no one listening or considering her, that he appeared again. Serendipity put him just a two hour drive away, heart broken from his own marriage failure. This time she had done the healing; validating him as a person, and reminding him that someone cared. And then they had helped each other navigate the rapid waters of divorce, so they could live the life they both dreamed of together. It had been the ultimate fairy tale ending, just like in the book. But the Happily Ever After had been short lived.

Lori closed the book and hugged it close to her chest, looking across at the hospital bed. He had been so brave, her Prince, having fought the terminal liver cancer for more than two years when they had only given him 6 months. And looking at him now, with his beseeching eyes locked on hers, he made it clear he wasn't ready to give up on their fairy tale ending just yet.

# The Little People

*Leonard E. White*

In older days, the Wee Folk were courted by brave but foolhardy men who sought treasure and power. Those poor fools were tormented to madness and then left to die as the pitiful creatures they were.

Wiser people left offerings for the Fae. Showing respect to things they didn't understand. These people were rewarded in subtle ways for their generosity because the code of Sidhe demanded balance through the return of a favor.

People, who are not immortal, change with the passing of time. They forget the lessons of their grandmothers, and so the Fairies were forgotten. The Fair Folk were no longer believed in; though they were still among us.

John sat looking at the tiny plaster fairy that his daughter had made for him. It was lopsided and the wings were mismatched but that didn't matter. Hanna had molded it with tiny hands in a summer craft class and he would proudly display it on his desk.

Hanna had also borrowed a book of legends from the library. So after learning about the fairies his little girl had begun setting out bread and butter every night. 'It's just a matter of time until the coons that are eating that bread start tipping over the trash cans,' he thought as he sat the little statue beside his daughter's picture.

She had made him promise to feed it. To leave something out at night for the fairies who would come to see the small lump of clay. So he had, and now, as he prepared to head home for the night, John felt a little silly placing a cracker at the statue's feet. The important thing to him was the promise. He taught by example and it wouldn't do to lie to his daughter.

He would keep his word.

The next morning, John stood outside his cube in wonder. The cracker was gone. He would later decide that the night crew had thrown it away but he wouldn't think about that for hours. He was too dumb-founded by the beautiful, fresh-cut flowers that were in his coffee cup.

# Three Simple Words

*Cory Eadson*

'I can't do this!' Anna cried to herself, gazing at a picture of that young, handsome man on her computer screen. Max. His perfect blue eyes, and shoulder length blonde hair promised so much, as much as his tender words, shared with her over countless phone calls and emails over the past four months.

'You can, my dear...' came a cheerful reply from behind her.

She turned her head to see Rael, her imaginary friend since childhood, perched on the windowsill with his arms folded as tightly as the black wings on his back. His piercing green eyes seemed to burrow into her soul.

'He's going to say those three simple words, I am certain!'

Anna shook her head angrily, wrenching her gaze from that infuriating idiot. How could a personification of her own inner-thoughts exude such confidence?

'But he hasn't seen the real me, hasn't seen...' Her voice faltered, as she brushed away a strand of brown hair to reveal a deep scar, trailing from the left side of her forehead down to her cheek; her left eye made of glass.

Rael's words stuck in Anna's head as she hurried through the busy town to meet Max for the first time. Her stomach was doing somersaults. How could Rael be so certain of Max's reaction? He was a guy. Guy's went for looks. She'd been bullied all her life because of the scarring, nobody had looked at her twice. Why should that change now? Because she'd told him her life story?

She found him, leaning against a wall outside a coffee shop, his eyes as blue as the sky. Her blood ran cold, and she wanted to turn and run, but too late. He'd seen her. He was already standing before her. His gaze already lingering on that badly-hidden scar.

Okay, she thought, blushing severely, let me down gently...

Then Max's eyes met hers, he smiled a big, broad smile. Then he leaned forward, whispered tenderly into her ear...

'You are beautiful....'

The three simple words she had always wanted to hear.

# Skin Deep

*Laura Jane Scholes*

The glasses had seemed unremarkable at best when an eight-year-old Belle picked them up in her grandmother's attic. The lenses were plain glass containing no prescriptions and seemed, to put it plainly, utterly useless. It was why her mother had allowed her to take them, thinking them nothing more than the object of a child's passing fancy.

When Belle wore the glasses to school the next day, her world shifted. The little girls in her class who mocked their poorer peers now appeared to her as ogres, their once luxuriant hair replaced by patches of stringy rat-tails. No amount of designer dresses could hide their ugliness and Belle shrank away, afraid. And it wasn't just the little girls. The vindictive children became small demons while the kind children had their goodness exaggerated. Their eyes were brighter, their smiles wider. They were beautiful in every sense of the word.

From then on, Belle wore the glasses. They protected her from those with cheerful smiles but dark intent and warmed her towards those with faces of thunder but hearts of gold. And then she met Adam. Adam, whose shyness and self-deprecating sense of humour told Belle he had no idea how wonderful he was. Behind the frames of her glasses he appeared as handsome as Prince Charming and she saw no reason to unveil his façade.

Though as time went on she did wonder what he truly looked like... and it wouldn't harm anyone if she were to sneak a peek. She loved Adam. His personality was beautiful no matter what. And so one day, under the pretence that the glasses were grimy, she plucked them from her face and turned towards her beloved.

Her smile faltered. Where her strapping Adam had been now stood a gangly young man. His face was pockmarked by vicious acne scars, his nose several sizes too large for his face, which only made his beady eyes all the more noticeable.

'Everything okay?' he asked.

'Fine,' Belle replied after a moment, putting the glasses back on. 'Just cleaning my glasses. It's difficult to see without them.'

# What Daddy Doesn't Know Won't Hurt Him

*Robert Fyfe*

Kerrie didn't really understand why her father would react so badly but she was determined that she would warn the fairies that he was coming to destroy them. All her life she had seen them but until yesterday her father had told her that she was making things up and to stop these fantasies.

She wished she hadn't lost her temper yesterday, hadn't been so determined to prove him wrong, but after all it was his fault that her two sisters had gone; he had driven them away to goodness knows where. She had promised the fairies that she wouldn't tell and they had shared their fairy dust with her. She had gotten so angry when her father had grabbed her, telling her that fantasies and fairytales were just make-believe and she should be real and forget them.

She had become so upset and had pulled the little bag of dust from her pocket, had sprinkled a pinch of dust over her head and had whispered the magic word; she had risen off the floor about three feet as she had looked into her father's eyes. So proud, so righteous, so in trouble.

He had grabbed her and threw her in her room telling her not to leave for any reason till he got back. She had heard him in the shed and she knew he was looking for a weapon against her friends.

He hadn't realised though that the fairy dust was still powerful and she opened her window and flew out of the room and down to the bottom of the garden, his screams for her to return easily heard as he came from the shed and saw her disappear behind the hedge.

The fairies were there waiting, laughing, arms open wide. Kerrie told them to run, told them to hide. But they came to her, held on to her. 'You just have to wish it away,' they told her. 'Just think about where you would like to go and we will all go with you. After all, it is what we did with your sisters.'

# Cooper and the Death-Cat

*Angela Goff*

Moosie the death-cat made another circuit at Woolsey Nursing Home. She sniffed the air at each doorway, tufted ears pricked and tail swishing, before moving on to the next room. The overworked, checklist-choked staff sometimes second-guessed when death was near. Not Moosie. She always knew.

'Tag on Judson, room nine,' said the aide to the nurse fumbling with her medicine cart.

'Moosie's in the door?'

'No - on the bed.'

On the bed. When Moosie took to someone's bed — you called in the family. The nurse left her medicine cart in the hall and peeked in room nine. Beulah Judson was upright in her hospital bed, talking to her toes.

'Don't look at me like that. Cooper wouldn't like it.'

As usual, thought the nurse (they never had learned who Cooper was); but where's Moosie?

An angry hiss answered her from beneath the bed. There she was -under the bed, not on it. Her back was arched, fur bristling, tail straight as an arrow.

'I'm not leaving yet. Cooper promised.'

The nurse pricked up her ears. Beulah Judson wasn't usually this lucid - even when she did talk to Cooper. And what was wrong with Moosie? This was not her usual bedside manner. Hiss. Scratch. YOWL. Scrambling beneath the bed – a blur of striped fur – and Moosie flew from the room, screeching like a banished demon.

'Cooper! Leave the cat alone!' scolded Beulah.

Another voice lilted through the room - a cool, sprightly voice that nonetheless sent chills up the nurse's spine.

'The cat was here to take you,' said the voice. 'I thought you weren't ready to leave.'

'Damn you, Cooper! What took you? I've waited decades.'

'Too many changelings, not enough children.'

'I'm too old to changeling,' said Beulah, while the nurse looked wildly about for the source of the voice.

'To have a changeling,' the voice - Is that Cooper? - said. 'And you're never too old to trick the Others. Do you want out?'

'Hell yes,' said Beulah.

'Then how will you leave?' said Cooper. 'By death - or changeling? We could use you, you know.'

# The Thing about Red-Hot Iron Boots

*Debra Providence*

The thing about red-hot iron boots is not that they are heavy, nor is it the heat. It's the fact that they are rusted iron boots glowing red. What sort of style sense went into making such a thing? Iron boots are passé. They reek retrograde and stink overindulgence.

Just like her and the way she's handling our tiff. She's married off; she's got her charming prince, although personally I've seen better looking and heard brighter speak, she's got her own new kingdom to add to the one she took from me. She's got the waterfall wedding dress, the towering cake and the piss those midgets conjured and called wine. She's got all these things, and still bears a grudge.

My guts rise when I think about the glut at that wedding. But that is how it has always been with her. Proclivity to excess, that one. She couldn't live with just one midget; she had to hoard seven of them, and to watch them tumble over themselves for her, like nesting dolls, like she was gold, or something. She doesn't have a heart of gold, I'll tell you that - all show and shine.

Overdramatizing everything, like with the apple.

I'll admit I let the brat get to me, but I didn't put that much belladonna on the blasted apple, just enough to knock her out a bit, to miss her passing prince. It was the least I could do for all the trouble she'd caused over the years. But she escalated it with the fainting, the pretending to be dead, and the glass coffin thing, because everyone would want to see a dead person's face as it turns to straw. So tasteless.

Now she's congratulating herself for picking the red-hot iron boots when she's really not got an original bone in her body.

Dancing in these boots won't kill me. They are heavy and they crush my ankles. They are hot and sear the flesh from my bones. No, instead it will be death by 'gaudy' for me. Red-hot iron boots indeed!

# Otter becomes a Bard

*Cameron Lawton*

All her life, Otter had wanted to be a bard. She knew that being a fishmonger was a good trade, but she wanted to be a Bard, she wanted to sing and tell stories to enchant others.

Sometimes she would hide in the reeds of the riverbank and harmonise with the birds that lived alongside – they were not the greatest of songsters, the ducks, herons, woodpeckers and jays, but they sat of an evening and made music for their own entertainment.

A bard, however, must know history – so Otter sat under the trees and listened to them talking, she dived into the river and let the water talk in her ears. Rather than just swimming through the water, she let it tell her of its life, the mountain snows where it had come from and the sea where it was going.

But the wise ones, the owls, clever creatures, all hooted with laughter and told her that bards were not fishmongers.

One night, the animals gathered together for the solstice, each to their own stone, in a circle, facing the centre where the moonlight shone and the Spirit made herself known. Something moved the otter to stand on her hind legs. She sang – sang the song of her river, the trees who had stood for hundreds of years, the stones under which she made her holt.

As she sang, each creature joined in, until all life offered up one song – birds, insects, mammals, the stones and trees, all of creation offered up one song of Solstice to the Spirit and a ribbon of multicoloured hue rose from the earth to the sky to tie them together. And in that moment the clouds covered the face of the Moon apart from one beam that shone on the otter to make a circlet on her head – the gold of a grateful Queen to her Bard.

Standing on her hind legs, her forepaws clasped to her chest and her eyes closed, the otter swayed to the music and knew that she *was* a bard.

# The tooth is out there

### Bernadette Davies

'So what you do, is put your tooth in your slipper, and leave it for the tooth fairy to come take away in the night,' Rachel explained to Matthew, who had just lost his first milk tooth and was jumping up and down with excitement at the prospect of earning his first 20p.

Matthew ran upstairs and proudly put the tooth in the slipper as his mum had instructed. Then, slipping the slipper under his bed, he made sure that Rex the dog wouldn't steal it before the tooth fairy had a chance to collect and leave his little money treasure.

Rachel smiled to herself as she watched Matthew descend from the stairs, who was grinning to himself as if he had just completed a very serious mission.

'Now remember Matthew, the tooth fairy wont come if you are not sleeping.' She made sure he understood, for she knew that with all this excitement it would be hours before he finally fell asleep.

'I think I will go to bed early tonight Mommy,' Matthew said. 'Can I have my bath now?'

'Of course.' Rachel smiled and they both headed upstairs.

At 7.30am the next morning, Rachel's alarm clock went off and, rolling over, she nudged Peter. 'Did you remember to put 20p in Matthew's slipper last night before you came to bed?'

'No,' Peter replied, 'I thought you were doing it?'

'Oh no!' Rachel exclaimed and jumped out of bed hoping that with any luck he would still be sleeping.

Tiptoeing towards Matthew's bedroom Rachel could hear him talking to himself. Dread washed over her as she realised how disappointed he would be thinking that the tooth fairy had not remembered him.

Slowly she opened the door and peered inside.

Matthew was sat giggling on the bed, happily counting out his money. Looking up and seeing Rachel he exclaimed, 'Look how much money I got Mommy!', and he held up what seemed to amount to £1 worth of change to her.

Puzzled, Rachel opened the door all the way so Peter could also see and asked, 'Are you sure?'

# Sleeping Beauty Undone

*Meg McNulty*

*True Love's Kiss the Spell Shall Break*

The rusty sign swung outside, creaking. An obscure picture, some sort of wheel.

'Spinning,' Emmie's pa muttered. 'Wool on your fingers... a real craft.' The room stank of cider and self pity, crushed cans leaning crazily against his broken chair. He was nostalgic now; within an hour he'd be violent. Time to get out. Dragging her cloak around her shoulders, she left.

It was just like every other home in Thorn, the shanty town that had sprung up in the shadow of the grief-stricken palace. Fairies. Emmie hated fairies. Trouble-causing, princess-stealing, lumps of vile magic. Witches were at least human. You knew where you were with a witch. Trapped in an oven, probably.

Her Pa had been a big man, red faced and loud. Singing, always singing as the wheel spun. A master spinner. Top of his game. Larger than life. Before Maleficent and the curse. Before every spinning wheel burned. Lost in her thoughts, she didn't see the horse until it was nearly too late.

'Watch out!' The rider sprang down, face white with anger. Or fear. Hard to tell. 'Damn you, do you have a death wish?'

God, he was beautiful. Rich too, with a silk tunic and skin like only royalty have. Clear and fine, not sun bronzed, not rough.

'Yes,' she said. 'Yes I do.'

That shut him up. He stared at her. 'You don't mean that.'

Emmie laughed. 'Don't I?'

Looping the reins over his arm, he held out his hand. 'Walk with me?'

'Is that a royal command your highness?' Acid in her voice, bitterness.

He threw her an odd glance. 'If you like.'

They walked for hours. Walked through Thorn and into the forest, past streams, through glades.

Past a golden haired girl, singing.

The Prince didn't even glance at her.

The next day they found Emmie's pa dead, choked on his own vomit. But when they looked for Emmie she was gone. Last seen on the back of a white charger, smiling. That night sleep settled across Thorn, across the Palace. Eternal sleep, never disturbed.

Not even by a kiss.

# Home Cooking

*Sara Leggeri*

She heard their tiny footsteps crunch in the snow. Both had blond coats and shiny green eyes. She cackled with delight, firing up the oven and the stew pot. She pulled the corner of the curtain aside. There they were, peeking from behind a tree. Her plan worked, she thought. What better than a house made of candy and frosting to lure them. They were the first to come in weeks. And two at the same time… She licked her lips.

She heard them giggling right outside the door. They had frosting all over their hands and mouths full of gumdrops. She grabbed the plate of cookies and opened the door.

They graciously entered her candy house with promises of all the sweets they could ever eat. She led them into the kitchen and locked the door behind them. Dinner will be grand. The boy has more meat, so he will go in the stew, and as long as the girl is basted while baking, she shouldn't dry out.

She started cutting vegetables over the stew pot.

She turned to offer them more sweets. They had crept behind her with devilish expressions. They grabbed her feet out from under her, tossing her into the boiling water.

Dinner will be grand, they thought.

# The Blue Garden Shed

*Jenn Monty*

Women were not Cal's strong suit. For years he had struggled to find Ms. Right, taking stock in the notion there was 'someone for everyone' and 'plenty of fish in the sea'. He had been to the bars, tried the online dating thing, he had even let his co-worker set him up on a blind date. And yet there he was; 33, with no real relationship experience. It wasn't for lack of trying; women just didn't seem to relate to him. His Whedonisms and obscure comic references seemed lost on his dates. They were unimpressed by his processing speeds and redundant backups. And none had every fully appreciated his blue garden shed in which he had cleverly designed a basement in order to make it deceptively bigger on the inside.

So it was with a blatant lack of interest that he clicked down the blinds to peer out the window at the sexy new neighbor moving in next door. The curvy figure was enough to make any man take notice. But it was the trash blonde hair and cut-off shorts that had Cal's fantasy machine cranked into overdrive. Maybe she was a model; or she might be an exotic dancer. Better yet she could be an undercover CIA agent stationed there to keep an eye on the local motorcycle gang. Except Cal wasn't sure he had ever seen a motorcycle gang, much less one in the area.

Cal watched until the last box disappeared into the recesses of the house along with his mysterious neighbor. He reluctantly let go of the blinds and resolved to get back to his Saturday; his lawn wasn't going to cut itself. After 30 grueling minutes of pushing a mower around his small yard, Cal headed into the back lost in thoughts concerning his next Skyrim mission. He failed to notice Ms. CIA eyeing him from her back porch so he almost tripped over his own feet when she said hello. His bottom jaw hit the ground when she nodded toward his blue shed and said, 'Nice TARDIS. Is it bigger on the inside?'

# An Introduction to the Arabika Manuscript Fragment by Professor Conan Floodqvist. (Published in the Journal of Pre-Event Literary Studies, June, 2157)

*Mark Wilson*

'Once Upon A Time.'

These are the only words that remain on the manuscript fragment PE459-6784-GY, discovered in the Voronya Caves by Spence Rocklin in 2149, although we know from the casing that it was 'A Fairy Story'.

The four words may seem meaningless in themselves, and though, post-Event, we only have other recovered fragments from the Old Times to go on, it may yet be possible, speculatively, to grope towards some conclusions, or inferences.

In particular, the word 'Once' sits uneasily with 'A Fairy Story'. We know, from Dr. Simone Tactitcia's analysis of the Aquitaine Cache, some of the depth of the history of tales of the faerie, and some of their characteristics, and the idea of such a tale being told only once will sit uneasily with modern readers. From what we have gleaned, the point of these tales, to those who lived before the Event, was that they were retellings of the inherent history of the world. For such a tale to happen only once is surely significant.

The word 'story' will likewise give some readers move to pause, but, as we know from the work of Robertson et al: in the Old Times, 'story' could simply mean a history that was told.

Too, the use of 'a time' rather than the (presumed) title defining a specific chronological location for the story may be a clue to the temporal instability that preceded the Event (and which has led to the recent discrediting of, e.g., Wilson's work on the Pembrokeshire Hoard), but the fact that this fragment tells of something that happened 'Upon', rather than 'during' or 'at' a time, is surely telling.

In fact, given how closely science has dated this fragment to the Event, could it be that we have discovered, somehow, impossibly, a fragment of the true nature of the cataclysm of those days, that wiped out history and changed our world? Was the Event caused by Fairies?

# Cinderella's Stepmother

*Denrele Oqunwa*

You must not believe all the tales they tell, those Brothers Grimm. For in the end, they are nothing but peddlers of second hand tales to frighten small children into docility.

No, if you want the truth, I can tell it. After all, I am Cinderella's stepmother.

Cinderella's father was not the sort of man to be long without a wife. He was fine and strong, and had wealth enough, but none of the town's women would consent to marry him because of that poor mite, his daughter.

But I had a soft heart, a fierce liking for the dashing Eduardo, and nothing but compassion for the child, out of her head though she was. I did not know the full extent of my burden until we were wedlocked, tied and true.

The child would not be tamed, talking to herself all hours of the day and night. She would not wash or brush her hair. She insisted on wearing rags as though they were coveted silks and cast away the fine dolls I bought her to scuttle around the cellar with the mice.

I tried my best to abide her ways, but in the end - my patience shot - I do confess I locked her in there and left her to her madness.

The ugly sisters? All in her mind. The prince? It is true his highness passed through once and stayed a fraught night, scared half to death by her nocturnal caterwauling and chittering. Come morning, he could not leave fast enough. Eduardo and I stood by shamefaced, making excuses of feral cats and vermin.

In the end, it was Eduardo himself who had her taken away, to a home that looked after her sort. As time wore on and the visits dwindled, I honestly was glad of it.

Upon her leaving, it was as if a shroud had been lifted. The house was at once filled with light and laughter and soon enough I was with child. A boy. We called him Charming, for he was bonny, mild and sweet.

And yes, we lived happily ever after.

# Fairy Dust Falling

*Veronica Stewart*

Was it real? Did I really see that? Day dreaming again? Well possibly, since I spent most of my real life wishing I was in the other realm where fantasy, as we know it, is indeed reality.

Getting down from the tree, I caught sight of it again, gossamer wings flashing against the moonlight. In a flash it was gone. I spent a lot of time in 'my' tree, I felt closer to my dreams up there somehow. Now I know for sure that this is not normal behaviour for an 11-year-old girl who should be skipping ropes and playing dolls, but I was Queen of the Fairies, really, and had been sent to my family by mistake.

Now I sit in my tree waiting for the Fairies to take me back to my Faerie kingdom, as they didn't know where I'd gone, so I'm trying to help them find me by sitting in 'my' tree, waiting for the day I will resume my rightful place in Faerie land.

Again I see the flash of gossamer; I see faerie dust falling, falling on ME!! Can this be it? Surely it must be: my skin is sparkling as if dusted with diamonds... I'm falling, falling, falling... or am I flying? I am filled with expectation...

I'm on my way, aren't I?

# Beanstalk in a Box

*Tim Kane*

Ever yearn to journey to the clouds? Intrigued by those darned cumulus ogres? Well, be curious no more. The new Beanstalk in a Box is available from Feefie Foofum Enterprises. This splendiferous invention will transport* you and your friends to the magical cloud realms above.

The price for a Beanstalk in a Box is one cow. (Due to the fact that bovines are difficult to acquire in urban areas, we will accept a cow-equivalent: seventy-five pounds of beef, four hooves, and one sweet bread.)

Your Beanstalk in a Box will arrive with three magic beans, each preinstalled with three cloud destinations (Cumulus, Stratocumulus, and Cumulonimbus). Please plant your beans outside in an open area** and leave overnight. Once your beanstalk has risen to cloud level, it is ready to climb. Despite the weather conditions in your area, be aware that temperatures in the troposphere can be downright chilly (-40°F), so bundle up.

CAUTION: When you reach your desired height, step onto the cloud using your cumulus clogs only. Failure to do so will result in insubstantial cloud buoyancy***.

Please be advised that ogres tend to frown on thievery. Consider a moment how you respond when ants scramble into your abode and make away with your food. You coat them with bug spray. As a cloud traveler, you might be interested in purchasing the optional gas mask rated for level 3 toxicity.

Exciting news, our beanstalks are now disposable! Yes, when you're done traveling, simply use the included hatchet to chop the beanstalk down. Please allow five miles of open land for the disposed beanstalk to fall****.

Remember, souvenirs from the cloud realms are not allowed. Should an irate two-ton ogre follow you down, you may be tempted to cut the beanstalk right away. This will cause the ogre to plummet toward you and your abode. Listen Jack, don't say we didn't warn you.

---

* Users will need to climb the beanstalk.
** Allow 12 feet on all sides. Not responsible for root damage to dwellings.
*** Falling.
**** Yelling 'Timber' does not protect from potential lawsuits.

# Goethel's Tower

*Stacy Bennett*

For years, I traveled the reaches of space, dreaming of a beloved smile and sorrel hair that craved tousling. That's over now. I drop out of warp dangerously close to the lofty landing towers that encircle Goethel Station like a crown of thorns. Lurking behind the huge freighters that wait to dock, I scan the radio chatter patiently.

Years ago, my people were subjugated, pressed into service, altered. Cyborg interfaces and enhanced reflexes make me the quintessential pilot and fighter, but cyborgs aren't citizens, merely property. I've heard out on the Rim no one cares what you are. It's a dangerous place, but you're free.

'Rappel Unit - Zebra Echo Lima. Snare initiating,' comes over the radio. I remember that voice.

Luminous strands slither out from a Tower. Like glowing hair, they twirl around a nearby freighter, snaring it, drawing it to a safe berth. Flying under the golden strands, I sneak along them to the Tower. Designation: RapUn-ZEL.

Z-E-L.

Zachary Edward Lanier: My husband, once upon a time. My ship lands vertically, grappled to the side of the tower. Connecting the ship's airlock to a maintenance access, I'm in. Goethel has forbidden the Towers to have outside contact, but I'm trained for stealth. Easily overriding the door mechanism, I enter the sanctum.

'Hello?' A distant raspy voice, but still him.

'Zach!'

A wheelchair approaches cradling a crippled parody of my love. Gone is the sorrel mop, hands thick-knuckled with arthritis. But Zach's soulful hazel eyes light up in his withered face.

'Molly?'

Shock singes my circuits. 'What happened to you?'

'Time.' His voice is soft with emotion. 'Ten warp years is much longer planetside, darling.'

I choke on life's cruelty. He aged while I dreamed and plotted. How long he's waited for me to come.

'I was going to the Rim.' My voice fades, my happy endings crumbling. So frail. Could he even survive the jump now?

'Is that an invitation, my love?' His eyes are sure; he knows the risks. I nod.

He chuckles. 'I thought you'd never ask.'

Goethel will be furious I've stolen him.

# Dragon Tale

*Amanda McCrina*

The dragon and I regard each other.

His eyes are cold, unblinking. He wins the contest every time. He's small, about as long as my arm from fingertips to elbow. But the size doesn't really matter. I've heard stories about how quickly the beasts can move. In some stories it doesn't take more than their breath to kill you. I've already used up my only weapon, the pail I'd been carrying. Mother had sent me for water sometime last century. My aim was pretty bad. The pail just bounced harmlessly about four feet up the trail from where the dragon is lying. The water that was in it is already gone in the white-hot sun. So now I face him unarmed. His mouth is open wide to show pointed teeth, and he's hissing. I daren't turn away. I stand stock-still. A trickle of sweat has started down between my shoulder blades.

'You been standin' there long enough you could stick up your arms and folks'd think you was a Joshua tree.'

The voice comes from behind me. I whip my head around. A man has come down to the stream from the opposite bank of the arroyo, leading a milk-white horse by the reins. A boy, really - he isn't much more than my age. But he's got spurs on his boots, a gun holstered on his hip.

'Sorry, ma'am,' he says. He tips his weather-beaten hat to me. 'Didn't mean to startle you.'

'There's a dragon,' I croak.

'A dragon?'

I point. He brings his horse across the stream towards me, follows my finger with his eyes. The beast watches, still hissing, coiling up now, fixing to strike. The boy unholsters his gun, spins it in his hand with ease, lets off one quick shot. The dragon rears back and drops in a puff of dust and lies still, just like that.

'No match for Ascalon,' the boy says with pride. He holsters the gun again and pats the handle. He smiles at me, sticks out a hand. 'Name's George,' he says.

# A Single Rose

*Melinda Williams*

'A mere moment is what I seek.'

The girl with the tattered dress and worn shoes swept her eyes to the garden before shyly sweeping them back to the farmer. He gazed upon her, taking in the dirty brown rags meant to be her smock. Pity for the girl rose in his chest and he couldn't answer her right away. 'Sire, please...' she trailed. Grunting, the farmer impatiently motioned his hands toward the garden. The girl's eyes lit up with appreciation as she clasped her hands together. 'I shall not be long,' she told him quietly. He watched as she hurried through the iron gates.

'Father, why do you let that girl into our garden? She's but a poor waif and I'm not particularly proud of your display of charity,' the farmer's son haughtily said. 'Nor am I, son. Just watch and wait.' The young man crossed his arms and glared in the girl's direction with narrowed eyes. As soon as the girl approached the single rose in the center of the garden, a glow appeared around her. 'See? See there, boy?!' the farmer exclaimed in a hushed voice. 'It's the sunlight, father,' he answered dryly. He turned to see his father walking toward the girl. Before his eyes, a beautiful woman stood in the garden and the girl was gone. The young man squinted his eyes, trying to remember why she looked so familiar. He took a few steps toward the gate keeping his eyes on her.

'Mother?' he asked in a shocked voice. At that moment, the old farmer fell to his knees and began to weep for his wife. Thunder clapped in the distance causing the man and his son to look up at the sky. When they lowered their heads, they watched as the young girl in rags stepped out of the gate, turning once to wave with a new twinkle in her eye.

# A Tale of Morality (or is that Reality?)

*Gail Lawler*

Once upon a time - Ok, Ok, it's Flash Fiction, cut to the chase.

Goldilocks sat scratching her rear, the little bears chair wasn't as comfortable as the story had made out and whilst deliberating over the porridge her bum had gone decidedly numb.

Even the food wasn't up to much, she was used to Egon Ronay, well, at least four stars. It was OK being a celebrity but she was tired of all the three bears stuff and she wanted to move onto more serious roles. Sleeping Beauty for instance, she could do that, even at her age. Much more glamorous than messing around with smelly, old, flea infested grizzlies.

Anyway baby bear was now pushing 20; it was ridiculous, a grown bear dressed in a diaper, in fact the whole thing was getting a bit passé.

Still, a job is a job. She had been offered 'Big Brother' but had turned that down. Humpty Dumpty had gone in her place, and apparently it wasn't all it was 'cracked' up to be.

Goldilocks stirred the lumpy porridge, her dyed shimmering locks looking decidedly brassy in the glare of the electric light.

She sighed, all alone on a Saturday night, even the 3 bears wouldn't be at home tonight, they were performing their 'Bear Gees' tribute on 'Britain's Got Talent'.

Slumping back in her seat Goldy was just about to cry when she heard a loud knock at the door.

Looking up she could see the shadow of two ears and a snout through the window.

She smiled a little smile. It was Wolf. He must be on his way home from seeing Little Red Riding Hood. Well, it wasn't Prince Charming, that's for sure, but Wolf could be very charismatic if you caught him in the right mood.

Maybe he could take her to the local bar? The 'Pumpkin and Slipper' was having a 'buy one get one free' evening.

Straightening her dress, Goldilocks tidied her hair before answering the door.

Outside the wolf licked his lips, tonight could be the night for a little celebrity 'Come Dine with Me'!

# The Seer of Viceroy

*Melanie Conklin*

A lazy tradesman is driven out by his wife, and bidden to make something of himself. He comes upon a washerwoman who has lost seven milking cows in seven weeks. He promises to restore the cows and heads off in search. As he walks he asks the wind a favor.

'Mighty wind, you travel far and wide. There is no land you do not touch. Help me find these missing cows, and I shall be forever grateful.'

At this humble request, the wind whispers in his ear the location of the missing cows. He follows the whispers, finds the cows, and returns them to the washerwoman, who rewards him with two bags of silver.

The tradesman comes upon two servants of the King. A pitcher of gold has gone missing, and he pledges to find it lest the servants be hanged. He spies a stream nearby, and once more he begs assistance.

'Mighty water, you travel far and wide. There is no crevice you cannot seek. Help me find the missing pitcher of gold, and I shall be forever grateful.'

At this modest request, the water gurgles in his ear the location of the missing pitcher. It has fallen deep within a well, and he fishes it out, and returns it to the King, who rewards him with four bags of silver.

On his journey home, he meets a sage who says, 'Tradesman, you are so very wise. Tell me what I hold in my hand. I wager six bags of silver you cannot.'

The tradesman places his own six bags of silver into the wager. He is eager to double his fortune. He looks up at the sun, and once more asks for help.

'Mighty sun, your rays reach far and wide. There is no object you have not seen. Help me guess the item this sage conceals, and I shall be forever grateful.'

But the sun does not speak to him. Clouds obscure it from sight. In his despair he is unable to guess, and the sage collects his winnings, and tradesman is left with nothing.

# Cinderella 2: This Time It's Personal

*Andrew Barber*

'Well of course you're shallow!' said the Fairy Godmother. 'What's with the sense of entitlement? Of course you can't go to the ball. You don't belong. Why would you want to go? Have you got anything to wear? No! You expect me to provide it. Why do you want the prince? You've already got Buttons.'

'I don't want Buttons, I want the prince,' said Cinderella.

'I want, I want... it's all I get from you. Ooh, I have to have the best carriage and the finest horses and a ball gown that makes me look like a meringue so I can pretend to be someone I'm not. Don't you think someone wanted that pumpkin? And what did the mice ever do to you? You're just bloody selfish.'

'But you're my fairy godmother! You're supposed to be helping me!' She stamped her foot.

'I am helping you, you airhead! You'll get nowhere with these ridiculous expectations. Live within your means. Pick a man who loves you, not some tool who thinks you can base love on shoe size. Learn to be happy within your own life. Don't change your life. Change yourself.'

'Don't change my life? I have to work!'

'Everyone has to work, sugar. You think I'm doing this for the good of my health?'

'You don't know what it's like. Did you never watch Slumtown's Next Top Princess and think 'that could be me?''

A derisive snort. 'You need to sort your life out, girl. You're even harder work than Lady Di. And we all know how that ended up...' A shudder. 'Look, you need to get this into your head. You're not going to be a princess. Like most people, you've got a hard life that you have to make the best of. Work out what skills you've got and use them to your best advantage.'

So Cinderella got herself pregnant by a married footballer, sold her harrowing story to the tabloids and spent the rest of her life blaming the fairy because she wasn't a princess.

# Just the Ticket

*Eleanor Capaldi*

'Are you sure this is your ticket?' the cloakroom attendant asked me. Of course I was sure, I'd only been given it a couple of hours earlier. But my pal had pulled, and seeing as we were a two woman team, that left me decidedly on my own. Not that I wasn't happy for her, but it did take the fun out of dancing. Having no-one to dance with.

So, he asks me again, 'Are you sure?' Completely. My bag therefore missing, the hunt begins. While mindfully musing the practicality of a sweep of the building, I saw a flash of white heading out beyond the cloakroom and down towards the dance floor. A glance over the shoulder vaguely in my direction. Bitch had my bag.

I forgot my usual feeble approach in the face of danger and set off in hot pursuit. Within a couple of minutes I could just see the back of the person disappear into the civilisation of the crowd. Under the lights, white showed up in a sort of ghoulish glow, as if UV paint had been spilt all over the enthusiastic club-goer. I began to weave my way in and out of the maze, searching for spaces; under an elbow here, round a waist there.

Timidity began to grow. The flush of 'no fear!' faded as I steeled myself to meet my thief. I hoped they weren't bigger than me. Long legs poked out the edge of an alcove.

So she was bigger than me. Damn.

Dark jeans to slim body, encased in white shirt. Charm of necklace resting low. I followed the chain and it led to glinting hazel eyes, dark hair pinned back. Oh god she might be Mediterranean. Suddenly my head is imagining beaches and vegan paella and coffee on the veranda.

But I must stop. This is my thief. And there is her loot. My bag. Sitting quite peacefully beside her. Matching ticket number still attached.

She studies me in the eye, and before I can launch into any tirade,

'I knew I had to get your attention somehow.'

# Twisted Cinderella

*Raiscara Avalon*

Tina was tired of being hated. It wasn't always like that, when she was a girl she was cosseted by both her parents and there was so much love in the house it amazed Tina that the seams didn't split. That is, until her mother died in childbirth. They said her brother was stillborn. Her Momma died three days later, some said of a broken heart. Then Papa remarried to an evil harridan. Tina wasn't allowed to call her that; however, it was always 'Madam.'

The harridan came with three kids of her own, as she had been widowed for many years. She had two of the most selfish girls possible and a horrid son. Fortunately the son had established his own house after being at school for many years, so Tina didn't have to deal with him often. He made her extremely leery when he did come around, he had a gleam in his eyes that made Tina want to crawl into the nearest corner and hide.

She spent years as a servant to them. At first her Papa would take some of the burden off, make sure she was well fed and had decent clothes. But eventually even that stopped as Papa got more comfortable with having an unpaid servant around. She had enough of being kicked around like a dog, having the fact that she was half-fae shoved into her face like it was an insult and having nothing but rags to clothe her blooming body. So she started slipping arsenic into their morning and afternoon tea. Small amounts at first, but as time went on larger and larger amounts. Being half-fae worked in her favor, as she used what magic she knew to ensure that no trace remained on her hands or on the tea set.

Finally the glorious day came. She went upstairs to Papa and the Harridan's bedroom to wake them as she always did, and they were dead. Faking a scream, she dropped the tea to the floor and ran into the girls' rooms.

They were also dead.

She had done it.

# Maddie White

*Jo-Anne Teal*

Four days to cheque Wednesday and Maddie's broke. The money from February lasted two weeks, which was record-breaking, but now the rent's been paid and it's back to walking alleys, looking in restaurant dumpsters for food. As with most things in her life, she finds that timing is everything. If you don't get to the dumpster quickly, rats get dibs on leftovers. Maddie knows. She's fought with a few of them for donuts when she was desperate.

She pushes her bangs out of her eyes. Her thick black hair can be unruly so she wears a bowed red velvet ribbon to tame it. The ribbon was a gift from her father on her 17th birthday. It was the only present he ever bought her and Maddie figures he shot himself to get out of buying her another on her 18th.

Annaluk scores crack several blocks away and says she's brought some back for Maddie to make the day go faster. Maddie remembers too well the feeling last time Annaluk shared her stash, so says thanks, I'd appreciate it.

Laying down so Annaluk can shoot the day-hastening pain relief directly into her jugular, Maddie waits for the blissful feeling to overtake her. And for a few minutes, it does. But then, she starts to shake. Her ivory white skin turns ashen and the shaking turns into violent tremors. Annaluk calls down the alley to the medic team trolling the neighbourhood distributing clean needles, then runs off in the opposite direction.

Thirty-six hours later, Maddie stirs in bed, squinting in pained recognition she's in the hospital. Opening her eyes, she tries to focus on the face looking down at her. After several minutes she realizes the face she's staring into is a handsome one, complete with kind blue eyes. The intern smiles as he watches her closely. And then, as if anticipating the questions now rushing through her brain, Dr. Reg Alprince shows his hospital identification card, introduces himself and says:

'Welcome back Maddie. You've been asleep for quite a long time. I'm glad I was here to wake you up.'

# Lost Property

*Laura Huntley*

Gordon searched the carriages at the end of his shift, scooping up the weird and wonderful artefacts of lost property to hand into the station: a family photograph, a paisley scarf and a single jewel encrusted, glittering stiletto. He had a funny feeling in his crotch that he didn't understand, and so, uncharacteristically, stuffed it into his bag.

Back home, he took it out and lovingly stroked the knobbly crystals. It was a large shoe, he immediately visualised an outrageously tall blonde with a figure to die for. Gordon wished to find the owner. During the night, he dreamed about sliding his foot into the stiletto.

In the morning, Gordon did some internet research and discovered some photographs which looked just like the shoe he cradled in his free hand. He printed off the address and ran out to his bicycle. He arrived at Diane's Boutique and struck gold. She had recently embellished that very shoe, for Vicky over at Wonderland.

Gordon dashed over to Wonderland, a strip club with violet walls. He shyly asked to see Vicky; he wished to return some property left on a train. Vicky is a man, dressed as a woman. Gordon's level of excitement, concerning the shoe, does not falter.

'Oh my Prince Charming!' shrieked Vicky in a male voice. The long blonde wig confused Gordon. As did the fact that Vicky was outrageously tall and had a figure to die for.

'Would you like to go out for a drink some time?' Gordon heard himself asking.

'You're not my usual type,' stated Vicky. Gordon felt crushed.

'What's your usual type?' he asked.

'Gay!' laughed Vicky.

'I might be,' Gordon offered tentatively.

'That's for you to decide,' said Vicky, stooping down to kiss Gordon's bald patch.

'Show me,' Gordon pleaded, handing Vicky the majestic shoe at last.

Gordon had a front row seat at the Wonderland strip show. Vicky wore the jewel encrusted heels, was blonde, outrageously tall, and had a body to die for. Vicky also had the same body parts as Gordon.

Gordon was in love.

# The Woman and the...

A. Herbert Ashe

He loved her, and hoped that one day he could be in the house, sitting beside her. It was all he wanted, yet was certain it would never happen. His will was strong, and rooted in her tremendous beauty. He changed with the seasons, but his love was steadfast. Through unforgiving winters and scorching summers, he did what was expected of him. It was all he knew.

Every time she left the house, she walked right past - and never gave a second look. To see her was reward enough for all he did. Her hair was soft, and nestled itself into every breeze, and her eyes sparkled in the sunlight, like morning dew in a field of grass. He lived for the moments she glanced in his direction, even if it wasn't to look at him.

Just once, even if just for a moment, he wanted her to notice him, smile, and welcome him into her home the way she had to so many of her friends.

It was New Year's Eve, and she hosted a party. Most came in couples, and all enjoyed music, food and wine in anticipation of the midnight celebration. As the wine continued to flow, some eyes started to wander. Winks and smiles were exchanged behind unsuspecting backs, and secret messages were being sent from phone to phone. A long absence by her date prompted her to get up and find him. She found him, in a back room of the house, kissing and caressing one of her house guests. Filled with a bit of wine herself, she pried them from one another, and rushed them both out of her front door, hoping never to see either one of them again. Sensing her embarrassment, and realizing the party could not recover, her friends quickly grabbed their things and left.

She walked off of her porch, leaned on him, and started to cry. Her tears ran onto him, just as the clock hit midnight. Suddenly, he had arms to hold her, and a head to rest on top of hers.

'Please don't cry.'

# Happily Ever After

*H. L. Pauff*

'Grandpa, please, please, please tell me a story.'

Charles pulled the blanket over his grandson and tucked it behind his shoulders as the young boy looked up at him with wide eyes.

'Oh alright,' Charles said, stroking his chin and kneeling by the bed. 'Hmm...Let's see...Once upon a time there lived a very brave and very strong and very, very handsome man who lived in a great big castle with his wife who was the prettiest and fairest maiden in all the land. They loved each other deeply and had not a care in the world until one day when the brave man was called on to protect his... kingdom from very bad guys. He left his wife and his young children behind to travel to a faraway land to fight the evil doers.'

'What did the bad guys do?' the young boy asked.

'They locked up innocent people and tortured them,' Charles answered.

'Did the brave man beat them up?'

'He sure did. They had great big mechanical monsters, but they were no match for the man. He fired his... magical beam and made the bad guys pay. He freed the people and they loved him. When it was time to come home, his kingdom threw a big welcome back party for him. He rode in the streets and people cheered for him as confetti fell from the skies.'

'Whoa, that's awesome.'

'He was a real hero,' Charles paused and looked at the floor, 'But when he went home to see his wife and family after many years he found another... bad guy in his castle with his wife. It seemed that being away and serving your... kingdom was not enough for his wife to stay... safe from the bad guys.'

The little boy's eyelids became heavy, but he saw his grandfather's fists clench and heard the hollowness in his voice.

'What happened? I bet the brave man saved his wife and they lived happily ever after,' the young boy said through a yawn, closing his eyes.

'Of course...' Charles whispered as he turned off the light and wiped a tear from his eye.

# The Guardian

*Rebecca Fyfe*

Cassie found a fluffy orange cat in the bushes outside her bedroom window. He was growling and hissing and looking very grumpy. He was huddled under her bushes and he looked as if he'd been through a fight. He had some small cuts and he was dirty with lots of twigs and leaves stuck in his fur.

She couldn't leave him like that, so for the next hour, she coaxed and cajoled, trying to get him to come out to her. Finally, with the help of a can of tuna from her kitchen cupboard, she managed to get the dirty and hurt cat to come out from the cover of the bushes. She left him eating the tuna and was surprised when she got up to go inside her house and he followed her right in.

Later that night, as Cassie slept, her window flew open and the dark creature entered. It had been watching her for days. She was destined to fight his kind, blood suckers, evil fae and demons alike; her birth had been foretold centuries ago. But he would stop her before she ever even came into her power.

A cat lay at her feet and he pushed it aside as he closed in on her. He leaned in close over her, preparing one long, sharp fingernail to slice her throat. That's when he felt the burning pain of the silver sword pierce his heart. He turned, surprise on his face and saw a boy standing behind him, sword in hand. 'Where did you come from?' he whispered as he fell into eternal sleep and his body crumbled into dust.

The boy put the blade back into its scabbard. He leaned over, giving Cassie a gentle kiss to her cheek, and slowly shifted back into the rough orange cat he had been moments before. He jumped back onto the bed and settled against Cassie's leg. He would protect her. It was his duty.

# An Unlikely Fairy Tale: We're Going to Disney World

*Rachel Stanley*

Looking for specific people online can seem stalkerish, obsessive. Then you find a boy from your past that likes different movies, books, but they're still the same ones you like. Seems like kismet. Fate. Meeting him again makes you wonder even more. Long distance relationships get such a bad rap. They never work out. But it'll never happen. That stuff only happens in the movies. But then we find that... spark. And thank the stars up above it's so easy to search for people online. We swear we won't grow apart again, that we won't drift again. We keep talking through e-mail, texting, phone calls. We meet up again the next summer, just as we had that first summer. We go to an amusement park and act like complete and total idiots. Leaves change to ruby, goldenrod, sunset orange. Caught on fire. Fall break in the mountains of Virginia. Official 'couple.' Heavily frosted lawns, iced branches, bitter winds. Christmas isn't white, but it's a good one. Mutual visiting and celebration of completed finals. Birthday. Valentine's Day. Explosions of color. Azaleas. Dogwoods. Bradford pear. Wisteria along the highway. Spring break in Virginia. He says he'd like to get me a ring but doesn't have enough for one right now, will I accept his class ring? I say that sounds like something out of a movie, or a country song. He laughs because he hates country. I give a longsuffering, sarcastically dramatic sigh. Yes, I'll accept it. Summer. Beach. Bridal magazines in the sunshine. Smiles. We're going to Disney World.

# Once Upon a Time

*Mike Manz*

'Well it figures, doesn't it? It just bloody well figures.'

Larry sighed as turned slowly in front of the mirror, trying to see himself from every angle. The jet black of the jacket set off the gold highlights in his wings, his hair was styled perfectly; he was one dapper looking fairy. He twisted his shoulders to look at the back of his ensemble.

'What was I thinking?'

He'd panicked - no ifs, ands or buts. He'd panicked and now he'd be a laughing stock, and he really had no one to blame but himself.

It had happened yesterday when Susie Farnsworth, a centaur, had asked him if he was going to the senior prom. He'd said that of course he was going and then she'd uttered those five fateful words - 'Save a dance for me' - before trotting off to advanced math class. A dance. Dancing. There would be dancing at the prom. Larry hadn't the first clue how to dance.

He'd panicked. He'd cut out of school and headed downtown to one of the seedier districts where you could buy just about anything, and for cheap. Cheap was all Larry could afford. He'd bought a spell from a nasty old Hag that, she'd assured him, would teach him how to dance while he slept. Before bed he'd dutifully read the incantation and performed the gestures exactly as the Hag had described. He'd even managed to swallow the entire noisome potion that she'd given him for 'extra potency'. And then he'd gone to bed.

If only he'd read the label he'd have known that the Hag had given him the wrong scroll.

When he'd woken up in the morning, there it had been, apparently happy to see him. He'd had to cut a hole in his trousers just to put them on. Now here he was, with his senior prom just two hours away. He still didn't know how to dance and he looked ridiculous. Never mind the prom; he couldn't even go out in public like this.

For goodness' sake, who had ever heard of a fairy with a tail?

# Prairie Wishes

*Eric Martell*

There are a lot of wishes made in rest stops.

'I wish I hadn't gone to Taco Bell for lunch.'

'I wish I could stay awake without amphetamines.'

'I wish my kids would just shut up for one goddamned mile.'

At most rest stops, all except one, the wishes are answered in the more-or-less random way wishes are answered everywhere – that is, as a matter of happenstance.

Between mile markers 197 and 198 on a nondescript highway crossing a nondescript state lies the 'Heart of the Prairie' rest stop. Most people speed past it; some stop and use the restroom or take a nap or buy a terrible cup of coffee.

The custodian at the Heart of the Prairie is an older man, slow, plodding, and the one who puts up the 'Restroom Closed for Cleaning' sign that suffering travelers curse. The name tag on his faded grey shirt reads 'Gene' in pretend-fancy script, and he is a three-dimensional projection of a nineteen-dimensional being whose name in his own language, oddly, is Gene.

Bobby Jones was having a bad day. He'd been fired. Again. The envelope marked 'Final Notice' was on the floor of his car. And his last dollar was in the mother-loving candy machine, but the candy was stuck in the twisty coil. Sometimes a man is brought to the end of his rope by the smallest of things, and he could take it no longer.

Bobby fell to his knees in front of the scratched faux-wood panel keeping him from his Whatchamacallit bar and wept. He wept for all the paths his life had not taken and all the choices he had not made. But mostly he wept for that candy bar.

'I wish, just once, I could have something go right. Just one time.'

Mopping the red ceramic tile in the lobby, Gene heard Bobby's wish. He moved the mop forward, left, and back, and heard the hollow clunk behind him as the now-free Whatchamacallit bar fell from its perch.

He finished mopping the floor, secure in the knowledge that the universe was, once again, safe.

# 1002

*L.S. Taylor*

He slipped a rufie in my drink. Idiot me, I was already tipsy... It was New Years, and the club was packed. Going out alone like that? Yeah, not my best idea.

Now it was September 27th, more than two years later. Or so said my nightstand alarm clock's calendar. December 31st would mark the third year he'd kept me here.

Wherever this was. The Mojave, maybe? Something told me that despite the dry air and golden sand all around his stone fortress, I was still on American soil. I hoped. That was all I had left, you know?

'Scheherezade, my love.'

I gritted my teeth and looked away as he wrapped me in his arms. That was the price for having hippie parents. 'I've told you a thousand times. It's Sherry.'

See, Stockholm syndrome? Not really my thing.

He shook his head at me. 'No, dearest. Tonight is our thousand-and-first.'

I suppressed a snort. His gaze cooled, reminding me of the torture tools in the dungeon.

'Y-yes, darling,' I simpered. 'And what tale would you hear from me tonight?'

Once I was a children's librarian. Now I tell this nutjob stories.

'Your namesake,' he breathed, clasping my hands tight. 'Please.'

Nodding, I guided him to the bed. Our bed, unfortunately. Seated between him and the clock, I began:

'Once there was a sultan whose first wife betrayed him. In anger, he took a new wife to bed every night, then had them beheaded the next morning. Until Scheherazade. Each night, she told him tales, but she never finished before sunrise. Each morning, he would let her live so that he could hear the story's end. When on the thousand-and-first night she ran out of tales, she expected him to kill her, but the sultan realized he'd fallen in love instead. They were happy to the end of their days.'

'And you, love?'

I forced a blush. 'Of course.'

At that, he fell to nuzzling my neck, so passionate, so sure of himself. So foolish. I smashed the alarm clock against his skull.

Damned if I'd live with him another night.

# Fairy Lights

*Jean M. Cogdell*

The clearing came alive with fireflies everywhere. Lizbeth's eyes grew wide as one lit on her hand. She stood still as one became many. The bugs lifted from Lizbeth's hand hovering in the air, then launched to the sky. When the lights returned she stared in awe because they weren't alone.

Lizbeth wanted to touch these beautiful creatures flying with the fireflies so badly she quivered with excitement, without thinking she pushed her hand into the flying colors.

'Ouch.' Her finger was bleeding. She glared at the beings fluttering among the fireflies.

'Look what you did! I wasn't going to hurt you!' Lizbeth's shout blew the bugs in all directions. 'I should put you in a jar, that's what I oughtta do. Like the little bug you are; go around sticking people. Crap.' Lizbeth stepped back.

As Lizbeth watched, the tiny figure grew larger, almost reaching her waist. Perfect in every way like a porcelain doll and would've been lovely except for the scowl shooting daggers from those dark eyes. Lizbeth looked at the delicate hands holding the sword. Moments before that sword had done no more damage than a hat pin; now it could do a lot more than prick her finger.

To her right there more of creatures appeared, all in varying sizes. Lizbeth moved back, falling with a thud. The lovely firefly escort scattered leaving only the fairies surrounding Lizbeth. Gulliver's Travels popped into Lizbeth's mind; she hoped they weren't carrying ropes. Lizbeth found herself more intrigued than fearful for she could hardly take her eyes from the hypnotic flapping wings reflected in the moonlight.

'You're real. I'm sorry for scaring you. I wouldn't put you in a jar. Not really. But you shouldn't stab people.'
She eased up to her knees and crawled forward. The fairies heard the bells first, and then, Lizbeth caught the sound; Silver Bells. Their wings flapped once, twice and as if on cue all were airborne. Lizbeth sat back and the fairies soared heavenward vanishing into the night.

'They're real.'

# God Bless You, John

## Afsaneh Khetrapal

'I cannot court you any longer... I find that I'm not attracted to women.'

That had been what John had said to her. John, the gentleman who had been courting her.

And wasn't that good for her reputation? That she had no prospects and she'd converted one of the most eligible gentlemen in London. Iris forced out a sudden breath and lost her footing on the soil. Then she fell backwards, not a speck of her remaining dry in the icy pond her dress floated on. Probably looked like a soggy cream puff now. An angry one, after screaming into her bonnet like a lunatic before forcing herself out of the numbing water.

'Afternoon, Miss Smith,' came an amused voice. 'Enjoyed your swim?'

Reluctantly, Iris looked up at the jet black hair and granite eyes that were the irresistible Michael Connolly. Newly arrived from Bath and already to blame for a few hundred broken hearts, Iris couldn't say she was immune to his charms.

'Please go away.'

But she was not in the mood.

'Just met John?'

Her eyebrows rose in question and a rueful expression touched his face. 'I know what happened.'

'Then please leave.'

'It wasn't my fault. I thought he was just friendly,' he shrugged.

'What are you talking about?'

He raked a hand through his hair. 'Christ! He didn't tell you what he told me.'

'What?'

Michael's face flushed crimson. 'He said he loves me. John.'

'Of course,' she muttered.

'You're angry at me?' he said in disbelief.

'It isn't enough that every woman in the ton is in love with you? Now the only man who has ever taken an interest in me?' she yelled.

Silence struck his whole person then one step and their faces were almost touching. 'Not the only man,' he breathed, as he tilted her head up and captured her lips in a kiss that stole her anger. She leaned into his masculine warmth and sandalwood scent, then he wrapped his arms around her soaking frame and finally shook with laughter as he said, 'God bless you, John.'

# A Grim Tale

*Daniel R. Davis*

Jared's steps echoed off looming, moonlit buildings, their darkened windows like the eye sockets of grinning skulls. He had not planned on this walk home, or the trek down the alley, but a broken carriage wheel forced him into both, and now terror screamed silently that someone followed him.

A scrape echoed behind and he quickened his pace, clutching his cane like a club, or perhaps some magical warding device. Silly notion, he thought. He would have chuckled if he were not scared witless. His sister was the one who believed in such magical nonsense. He had never seen anything to suggest its existence and doubted he ever would. Shivering, he pulled his collar tighter and glanced over his shoulder, knowing that just as before he would find nothing.

The dark form struck, knocking him to the cobblestones. His spinning gaze rose to find a hoodlum looming over him, knife glinting, face a leering patchwork of teeth and shadows.

'Yer valuables,' the thief growled. 'Now!'

Jared tore at his frock coat for anything that might keep him from the business end of that blade. He found his money purse and pocket watch, thrusting both at the assailant, pleading.

Steel flashed, splashing dark streaks into the moonlit sky. The hoodlum gurgled, knife clattering away, his body slumping to the cobbles, a dark pool spreading about the feet of Jared's almost petite savior.

'Th...thank you!' he blurted, heart hammering. 'If you hadn't come—'

'Oh.' His savior turned, grinning, adjusting a faded stocking hat, red, Jared thought. 'Wasn't here for him.'

Jared's soul froze and he crab-walked to unyielding stone.

'Ye see,' the man continued, 'it's m' cap. 'Tis a bit faded, an' you're gonna help me fix it. It needs t' be red, an' I chose you. Needs t' be you, it does.'

Red cap's blade glittered, crimson coated, dripping. Clouds crawled over the moon, and Jared's final thoughts as glowing red eyes descended were of his sister and how he would never get a chance to tell her that at least one of those fairy tales were true.

# She Shall Go to the Ball

*Sarah Barry*

My sister had glided into the crammed sitting room. It was her Debs. She had looked radiant, no different to every other day; an array of faces was lit up by her conventionally stunning magnificence.

I suppose my inquisitive adventure had started soon after. My 17-year-old self had tried to discover if I held any worth. Everyone admired her, but could I get anyone to notice me? As it turned out everyone noticed me.

My expectant tummy got the attention of all around me and beyond. The catalyst was the waist band of my school kilt as it struggled to wrap itself around the two of us. It was the result of a month of hazy love and the incessant attentiveness of a first boyfriend.

The bright spotlight I had always craved just wasn't the type I had dreamt of. Afterwards I tried to retrieve the anonymity of the years I had spent in the sisterly shadows.

Lilly was 10 months old when my Auntie finally persuaded me that I still deserved to go to my Debs. She had lovingly cradled her second goddaughter, my baby, as she fixed a wisp of my hair that had escaped; her favourite perfume clasped ready to drench me.

My confidence had never really recovered from the vitriolic attention of my peers and their parents. Yet that night I caught a glimpse of a captivating 19-year-old in a purple satin dress. No crowds admired the scene as I opened the door to the boy awkward in his tux. Our eyes met and he looked amazed. Maybe he would be the one.

He was.

Today a hundred eyes bore into the flesh exposed by my ivory dress. Their warmth penetrates my every pore and I know it is real. The hateful absence of my parents is drowned out by the approval of my family, old and new. Lilly giggles as I hand the cluster of roses to her and my Aunt steadies my hand. His eyes meet mine once more, we sparkle.

I am a princess.

# Acknowledgments

As co-host of the contest and creator of this book, I'd like to give a few formal acknowledgments to the people who donated their skills, creations and time… Thank you to Diane J, Reed and Jessica Grey for generously donating copies of their beautiful books as prizes and for coming up with the perfect quotes for the cover; thank you to James Lennie for giving us the moon image and to Failed Artist for designing the t-shirt. A *massive* thank you to Fiveshock Design for designing and donating the gorgeous cover and for putting up with the painful reformatting process; and a big, big thanks to Lauren McMenemy who gave up a weekend to proofread all the stories (and found things that I didn't), and of course, thank you to Calum Kerr, Director of National Flash Fiction Day, without whom none of this would even have been thought of…

And last but not least, thank you to Anna 'Fairy Queen' Meade, partner-in-crime, enthusiast of all things – I hope you like the book ☺

*SJI Holliday*

# Author Information

You can find out more about the authors included in this collection via their links below.

Conor Agnew      www.twitter.com/ConorDA

Christine Anderton

Erin Ashby      www.spoonflipper.blogspot.com

A. Herbert Ashe      www.aherbertashe.blogspot.com

Raiscara Avalon      www.raiscaraavalon.wordpress.com

AJ Bailey      www.ajbailey.wordpress.com

Andrew Barber      www.firebeard-ravingsofamadman.blogspot.co.uk

McKenzie Barham      www.theothersideofsorrow.blogspot.com

Sarah Barry      www.relishingwriting.blogspot.com/

Oliver Barton      www.musicolib.net

Cath Barton      www.cathbarton.wordpress.com

Mary Benefield      www.mary-sparkofhope.blogspot.com

Stacy Bennett      www.ajaroffireflies.blogspot.com

Natalie Bowers      www.abutterflymind.tumblr.com

Jo Bromilow      www.redhead-fashionista.com

Eleanor Capaldi      www.twitter.com/brightstarshine

Molly Carr      www.amzn.to/KuWDw3

Barry Chantler      www.barrychantler.yolasite.com

Jean M. Cogdell      www.jemcogdell.blogspot.com

Melanie Conklin      www.melanieconklin.com

Chella Courington      www.gravityandlight.blogspot.com

Bernadette Davies      www.bernadette-davies.blogspot.co.uk

Daniel R. Davis      www.danielrdavis.com

Cory Eadson      www.morgue-of-intrigue.blogspot.co.uk

Mark Ethridge      www.mysoulstears.wordpress.com

| | |
|---|---|
| Annie Evett | www.annieevett.com |
| Tracy Fells | www.tracyfells.blogspot.co.uk/ |
| Rebecca Fyfe | www.imaginecreatewrite.blogspot.co.uk |
| Robert Fyfe | www.fairymagicgifts.blogspot.co.uk |
| Angela Goff | www.anonymouslegacy.blogspot.com |
| Jessica Grey | www.authorjessicagrey.com |
| Caroline Hardman | www.sowhodoesthat.blogspot.co.uk |
| J. Whitworth Hazzard | www.zombiemechanics.com |
| SJI Holliday | www.sjiholliday.com |
| Laura Huntley | www.laura-huntley.blogspot.co.uk |
| Mike Jackson | www.mjshorts.wordpress.com |
| Sarah Jasmon | www.sarahontheboat.blogspot.com |
| H. Johnson | www.gardenoftinyfiction.blogspot.co.uk |
| Tim Kane | www.timkanebooks.com |
| Miranda Kate | www.twitter.com/PurpleQueenNL |
| Angela Kennard | www.angwrites.com |
| Afsaneh Khetrapal | www.dreaming-of-stories.blogspot.co.uk |
| Veronique Kootstra | www.veroniquekootstra.wordpress.com |
| Kelley Lane | www.callmebookish.wordpress.com |
| Gail Lawler | www.5minutefiction.co.uk |
| Cameron Lawton | www.cameron-writes.blogspot.com |
| Sara Leggeri | www.saraleggz.wordpress.com |
| Dionne Lister | www.dionnelisterwriter.wordpress.com |
| Ruth Long | www.bullishink.com |
| Mike Manz | www.lived-inlife.blogspot.com |
| Eric Martell | www.twitter.com/drmagoo |
| Tamara Mataya | www.feakysnucker.blogspot.ca |
| Janina Matthewson | www.myrednotebook.com |
| Jessica Maybury | www.jmaybury.blogspot.com |
| Amanda McCrina | www.amandamccrina.com |
| LJ McMenemy | www.ljmcmenemy.com |

| | |
|---|---|
| Meg McNulty | www.darcytodionysus.com |
| Anna Meade | www.yearningforwonderland.blogspot.com |
| Jenn Monty | www.brewedbohemian.blogspot.com |
| A.G.R. Moore | www.agrmoore.blogspot.com |
| Jenn P. Nguyen | www.giveintotemptation-jenn.blogspot.com |
| Sarah Nicholson | www.re-ravelling.blogspot.co.uk/ |
| Denrele Oqunwa | www.braincandy.tumblr.com |
| Vicki Orians | www.vickiorians.blogspot.com |
| H. L. Pauff | www.hlpauff.com |
| Victoria Pearson | www.victoria-pearson.blogspot.co.uk/ |
| Nanette Pitts | www.gracepaigestoryland.blogspot.com |
| Debra Providence | www.debraprovidence.wordpress.com |
| Annabelle M. Ramos | www.annabellemramos.blogspot.ca |
| Angela Readman | www.angelreadman.blogspot.co.uk |
| Matt Reilly | www.twitter.com/mr_matt_reilly |
| Eva Rieder | www.evarieder.com |
| Fayne Riverdale | www.fayneflash.blogspot.com.au |
| Jessa Russo | www.jessarussowrites.blogspot.com |
| Laura Jane Scholes | www.justwaitforthestorm.blogspot.co.uk |
| Lisa Shambrook | www.thelastkrystallos.blogspot.co.uk |
| Rachel Stanley | www.2catchahummingbird.blogspot.com |
| Veronica Stewart | www.veronicastewar4.blogspot.co.uk/ |
| Jonathan Stoffel | www.inspirandomonium.blogspot.com |
| L.S. Taylor | www.lstaylor.blogspot.com |
| Jo-Anne Teal | www.goingforcoffee.blogspot.ca |
| Laurie Theurer | www.facebook.com/ltheurer & www.facebook.com/JackrabbitRanchandResort |
| J. Tsuroka | www.twitter.com/jtsuruoka |
| Keith Walters | www.booksandwriters.wordpress.com |
| Steven Paul Watson | www.stevenpaul-ashviper.blogspot.com |

| | |
|---|---|
| Leonard E. White | www.leonardewhite.wordpress.com |
| Melinda Williams | www.mindysue528.blogspot.com |
| Mark Wilson | www.underpleasanttrees.blogspot.co.uk |
| Jonathan M. Wright | www.jonathanmwright.wordpress.com |

*Life itself is the most wonderful fairytale of all.*
*~Hans Christian Andersen*

Printed in Great Britain
by Amazon.co.uk, Ltd.,
Marston Gate.